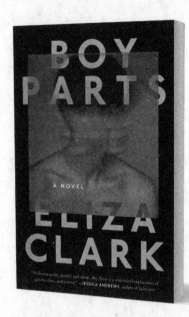

About the Author

ELIZA CLARK is the author of *Boy Parts* and *Penance*. *Boy Parts* was Blackwell's Fiction Book of the Year, and a stage adaptation of *Boy Parts* premiered at Soho Theatre in October 2023. Eliza has also been chosen as a finalist for the Women's Prize Futures Award for writers under thirty-five, named one of *Granta*'s Best of Young British Novelists, and listed on *Forbes*'s 30 Under 30 Europe. She also writes for film and television.

BILLIONAIRE'S CLUB

Bad Night Stand
Bad Breakup
Bad Husband
Bad Hookup
Bad Divorce
Bad Fiancé
Bad Boyfriend
Bad Blind Date
Bad Wedding
Bad Engagement
Bad Bridesmaid
Bad Swipe
Bad Girlfriend
Bad Best Friend
Bad Billionaire's Quickies

BILLIONAIRE'S CLUB CAST OF CHARACTERS

HEROES AND HEROINES:

Abigail Roberts (Bad Night Stand) — founding member of the Sextant, hates wine, loves crocheting

Jordan O'Keith (Bad Night Stand) — Heather's brother, former owner of RoboTech

Cecilia (CeCe) Thiele (Bad Breakup) — former nanny to Hunter, talented artist

Colin McGregor (Bad Breakup) — Scottish duke, owner of McGregor Enterprises

Heather O'Keith (Bad Husband) — CEO of RoboTech, Jordan's sister

Clay Steele (Bad Husband) — Heather's business rival, CEO of Steele Technologies

Kay (Bad Date) — romance writer, hates to be stood up

Garret Williams (Bad Date) — former rugby player

Rachel Morris (Bad Hookup) — Heather's assistant, superpowers include being ultra-organized

Sebastian (Bas) Scott (Bad Hookup) — Devon Scott's brother, Clay's assistant

Rebecca (Bec) Darden (Bad Divorce) — kickass lawyer, New York roots

Luke Pearson (Bad Divorce) — Southern gentleman, CEO Pearson Energies

Seraphina Delgado (Bad Fiancé) — romantic to the core, looks like a bombshell, but even prettier on the inside

Tate Connor (Bad Fiancé) — tech genius, scared to be burned by love

Lorelai (Bad Text) — drunk texts don't make her happy

Logan Smith (Bad Text) — former military, sometimes drunk texts are for the best

Kelsey Scott (Bad Boyfriend) — Bas and Devon's sister, engineer at RoboTech, brilliant

Tanner Pearson (Bad Boyfriend) — Bas and Devon's childhood friend, photographer

Trix Donovan (Bad Blind Date) — Heather's sister, Jordan's half-sister, nurse who worked in war zones, poverty-stricken areas, and abroad for almost a decade

Jet Hansen (Bad Blind Date) — a doctor Trix worked with

Molly Miller (Bad Wedding) — owner of Molly's, a kickass bakery in San Francisco

Jackson Davis (Bad Wedding) — Molly's ex-fiancé

Kate McLeod (Bad Engagement) — Kelsey's college friend, advertiser extraordinaire, loves purple and Hermione Granger

Jaime Huntingon (Bad Engagement) — vet, does excellent man-bun

Heidi Greene (Bad Bridesmaid) — science, organization, and *Twilight* nerd

Brad Huntington (Bad Bridesmaid) — travel junkie, dreamy hazel eyes, hidden sweet side

Ben Bradford (Bad Swipe) — quiet, brooding, had a thing for golden retrievers

Stef McKay (Bad Swipe) — lab assistant, dog lover, klutzy to the extreme
Tammy Huntington (Bad Girlfriend) — allergic to relationships
Fletcher King (Bad Girlfriend) — has a thing for smart, sassy women

Additional Characters:

George O'Keith — Jordan's dad
Hunter O'Keith — Jordan's nephew
Bridget McGregor — Colin's mom
Lena McGregor — Colin's sister
Bobby Donovan — Heather's half and Trix's full brother
Frances and Sugar Delgado — Sera's parents
Devon Scott — Kels and Bas's brother
Becca Scott — Kels and Bas's sister in law
Heidi Greene — Kels' friend since college
Cora Hutchins — Kels' friend since childhood
Fred — the bestest golden retriever in the world*Sir Fuzzy McFeatherston aka The Fuzz* — Jaime and Kate's pet rooster

To those with a past. We don't have to let it define us.

ONE

Abby

"IF YOU WERE A CHICKEN, you'd be impeccable."

I swirled the sip of rum and Coke in my mouth in an effort to not spit it all over the bar.

Then I swallowed carefully and rotated my head so I could see my friend Seraphina on the next stool over. She was currently holding court over a group of men.

Beautiful, tall, thin, and with a pair of boobs that could knock someone out—quite literally, they had once rendered a man unconscious. Okay, *well*, the sight of her impressive cleavage had caused the man to do a double take and promptly run into a large and extremely hard brick pillar in this very bar, but the point was still there. Seraphina was goddess gorgeous, and she was my very best friend.

"Get it?" the man who'd elbowed his way to the front of the crowd surrounding Seraphina asked. "Im-*peck*-able."

"She gets it," I muttered. "It's just so horribly im-peck-able that only an idiot like you would dare use it."

Seraphina's lips turned up at my caustic complaint.

"Hush, you," she murmured before raising her voice to address the man. "Puns. I do have a certain . . . *fondness* for them." Her reply started him talking, drowning on about different languages and double meanings. It might have almost been admirable, the sheer quantity of words orally puking all over our ears, if it wasn't so sad and pathetic.

Whew.

I took another sip of my drink. A bigger one because . . . *bitter much?*

"I'm sorry," Seraphina whispered out of the corner of her mouth. "I don't know why this always happens."

"You're Barbie," I said, bumping her arm with my shoulder. "It's not your fault."

My friend had that elusive *je ne sais quoi*. Unspoken charisma that drew men to her like flies to honey.

And if I was being honest, sometimes that made it hard to be her friend.

I didn't mind being in the background; I preferred it, actually. Given too much attention, I froze and inevitably made a fool out of myself.

But drawing a crowd of slavering men every time we went out made it difficult just to have a drink with my best friend, never mind a full meal.

"I'm sorry," she said again when Bad-Pun was displaced and another man slid forward in an attempt to claim Seraphina's attention. "I honestly thought the jacket would help."

I grimaced. "The jacket is what's doing it, I think."

A bomber made of black leather, it hit just beneath her breasts and managed to emphasize both the bounciness of that particular portion of her anatomy and the slimness of her waist.

"Next time, drinks at my place and takeout."

I saluted her with my glass. "Agree completely."

"Should we go?" she asked, tilting her head toward the door.

"No." I nodded at the Y-chromosomes dotting the space around her like flowers in a planter bed. "Prince Charming may be here."

One blond brow rose. "I doubt it."

"You're the one looking for a happily ever after." I nudged her arm with my own again, knowing my friend was a romantic and, despite her beauty, also very lonely. It was hard for her to find someone who saw her as more than the sum of her parts.

And Seraphina was desperate to be *more* for someone.

"I'm not so sure happily ever after exists," she said.

"Oh, it definitely exists." I held her stare, willing her to believe.

Because happily ever after *had* to exist.

For some people.

Of the goddess variety.

Because if Seraphina couldn't find it, then what chance in hell did I have?

Not that I was looking, thank you very much.

I was just fine with my laptop and my cozy socks and my books.

"Now get on finding that HEA," I said, using the code word from our favorite genre of books—romance, of course. Because what the heck was life without fictional eight-packs and alpha males who actually cared about the women they slept with?

Seraphina bit her lip and I narrowed my eyes at her. "I'll be here to quip nastily about all the bad pickup lines your prince tosses your way."

She laughed, leaned her head against mine. "You're the best."

I smiled, leaned back. "I know."

Seraphina turned back to her admirers and I pulled out my phone, half reading the latest release from one of our favorite authors, and half listening to my friend charm the socks off everyone around her.

"You're a good friend."

The male voice sent a shiver from my head to my toes. It was honey, warm and languid as it slid down my spine and sent my blood pumping.

Which was very, *very* dangerous.

I sighed. This was always the worst tactic, the most under-handed masculine effort to get my friend's attention.

Going through the slightly-rumpled, cute-but-definitely-not-gorgeous, exceptionally-clumsy best friend.

It sent my inner sidekick radar on full alert.

Mostly because I'd been hurt this way before.

So "mmm-hmm" was the only thing I said in response.

"Jordan." A hand appeared directly in front of my face, unfairly positioned between my booze, my book, and my eyes and mouth.

I huffed and finally looked up.

Then promptly felt my lips fall open. Because—*holy fucking shit*—this guy was gorgeous. Way out of my league, of course. But blond and blue-eyed and hard and tall and ripped. He brought every single Thor fantasy to life—the short-haired, shorn, lightning-bolts-on-the-side-of-his-head version.

Which, face it, was obviously the better variety.

He wore a pair of slacks and a gray button-down that was so sinfully tight around his biceps I half expected it to burst open. I studied those seams for signs of wear. I mean, a girl had to watch out for the rest of humanity, right?

Unfortunately for me, the shirt stayed in place and the signature lightning bolts weren't present in Jordan's hair, but his pants were so tight that his hammer—

I shifted on my stool, thighs unconsciously pressing together as blood pooled *there*.

Which was the exact moment that I remembered he wasn't there for me.

Damn.

He radiated that same allure as my best friend. Wasn't life just perfect sometimes? A gorgeous redhead was perched on the stool behind him, leaning forward in an almost obscene pose in order to compete with Seraphina's cleavage.

She couldn't, of course.

But it wasn't just one woman vying for his attention. No, they were dotted around the room, coquettishly blinking at him, crossing and uncrossing legs, adjusting outfits. Even the bartender—female, brunette, beautiful—had chosen to polish glasses two inches from his right elbow.

He was movie star handsome and he . . . was perfect for Seraphina.

"Abigail," I eventually made myself reply, putting my hand out to shake his.

It wasn't disappointment curling around my stomach. It couldn't be, not when Jordan was so stratospherically far out of my league.

He grinned—nice smile, *of course*—and shook my hand. I suppressed the zing of pleasure that coursed through me at the contact. Instead, I pulled back and hitched a thumb over my shoulder. "Her name is Seraphina. She likes cosmos and hates cheesy pickup lines, despite her kindness in accepting them." I decided to throw him a solid because, really, they were absolutely perfect for each other. "Talk to her about how much you love CSI."

I tucked my phone into my purse, grabbed my drink, and drained it.

"I hate CSI," he said, brows pulling down.

"If you want a chance with her, you might want to discover a newfound love for it."

My legs took a long time to reach the ground—short people problems—but luckily they'd made contact with the wooden surface before Jordan spoke again; otherwise, they might have kept on slithering until I was ass-down on the sticky floor.

"I don't want a chance with her," he said. "I want a chance with you."

My eyes flew up, and I couldn't help my breath from catching. I wanted that, too. A horizontal, writhing chance. Or hell, vertical. Semi-reclined. I'd take any of it.

My body was very aware of exactly how hot he was.

But then I remembered reality.

"I'm the best friend," I said and lifted my chin, forcing my words to be matter-of-fact. I'd been through this before. "You might be fuckable to the nth degree and perfect for Seraphina, but I refuse to set her up with a liar."

In a movement too quick for my brain to process, my stool was shoved to the side and I was pinned against the bar, heavy hips pressing into me, a hard chest two inches from my mouth.

Seraphina whipped around at the movement and I could just see her over Jordan's shoulder, her blue eyes concerned.

"Hi, Seraphina, I'm Jordan," he said, calm as can be, gaze locked onto my face then my eyes when mine invariably couldn't stay away. "I'm going to borrow your friend for a minute."

"Abs?" she asked, and I knew she'd go to bat for me right then and there if I needed her to.

"Weasel or no?" I managed to gasp out. For some reason, I couldn't catch my breath.

Not that it had anything to do with Jordan.

No, it had *everything* to do with him.

"Weasel?" he asked.

I shook my head, focused on my best friend. Weasel was our

code name for the men trying to weasel, quite literally, their way into my pants and then into hers.

I was just about ready to say fuck it—or me, rather—even if Jordan was a Weasel. He smelled amazing. His body was hard and hot against mine.

And it had been way too long since I'd had sex.

"No chemistry on my part—" Seraphina began.

"Your friend isn't who I'm attracted to," Jordan growled out. "You are, and it's fucking pissing me off that you don't believe that."

TWO

Jordan

THE WOMAN WAS CERTIFIABLE. How could a man even look at her friend when he could have *her*?

Silky brown hair, curves for days, lips that screamed to be kissed.

She was Jordan's every teenage fantasy come to life . . . and somehow she thought that he wanted her friend.

Insanity.

The friend, Sarah-something, nodded at him and he took advantage, tugging Abigail closer as he led them to the dance floor.

He didn't dance as a habit and certainly not after twelve long-ass hours in the office, which had been preceded by several weeks of the same. His workload was crazy at the moment. It had to be because he didn't trust anyone else with the specific details of the buyout.

Oh, he might let them do the work, even knew the company couldn't survive if he micromanaged every detail.

He just waited until they went home to double-check every single contract and calculation.

Jordan hadn't spent the last decade building his technology development firm only to be careless with the details in the home stretch.

And this was definitely the home stretch.

The beach, the surf, and a quiet house where he could get back to invention rather than management was his dream.

He was almost there.

Which meant he could stop and smell the flowers, right?

Or at least a woman who smelled like one.

Abigail fit into his arms perfectly, the top of her head coming just beneath his chin, her face pressing against his chest. He'd have to bend a bit to take those lips, but Jordan had the feeling it would be worth it. Plus, she smelled fucking incredible. Like a tropical island—floral with just the hint of the sea. His fantasy come to life.

She stepped on his foot.

Deliberately.

He smiled, loosening his grip as he glanced down at her. "Problem?"

Her eyes flared in annoyance, and Jordan had to give himself a mental slap to not kiss her right then and there. Those eyes were something special. Streaks of caramel and dark chocolate, gray and green and blue.

He'd never seen a pair of irises so unique.

And they were partially covered by narrowed lids as Abigail glared up at him.

"Why are you doing this?" she snapped.

Jordan grinned. "Why am I holding a beautiful woman in my arms?"

She stomped his foot again. "I'm not beautiful."

He snorted.

"I'm serious!"

"So am I," he whispered, bending so that his lips just brushed the top of her ear.

Her cheeks went pink, her lips parted, and her body wavered, leaning against his before pulling away. She was fighting him, but not because she didn't want him. There was something else underneath, an edge of panic that reminded him of a spooked horse.

"Shh," he said. "Let's just dance."

"But—"

He planted his feet, grasped her shoulders, and pulled her a full foot away from him. Enough to clear his head, enough to give her some distance if she truly did want to get away.

Crouching a bit to meet those gorgeous hazel eyes when hers wouldn't rise to find his, Jordan said, "Just a dance, flower girl, but only if you want it."

He knew he could be pushy sometimes, knew he was a fucking pain in the ass in the business realm, but he wasn't one of those guys who pressured a woman into being with him just because he wanted her. So what if she was gorgeous and her body was off the charts? Having a woman frightened of him wasn't a turn on.

Yeah, not really his style.

Plenty of guys in his universe used their power to get laid, but that had always disgusted him. What was the point in a woman being with him if she didn't want him as much as he wanted her?

Or because she wanted him for his ownership of a multi-billion dollar corporation or his fleet of private jets? Or, worse, because she was scared of the repercussions of *not* being with him?

And so he made sure Abigail knew that she could go.

But he also wanted to make certain that she knew *she* was the one he found irresistible—not her friend.

"You can go back over there to your drink and your book, side-kicking it with your friend, who may be model beautiful, but is also nothing compared to you."

She rolled her eyes.

"I'm serious. Your body is the one a man dreams of—curved and lush, not bony lines and hard angles. A man likes to cuddle with something soft, not a coat hanger."

Abigail glared at him then pointed to her friend and the group around of men surrounding her. "*They* like it. And Seraphina isn't bony, she's got huge—"

His mouth curved. "I'm more of an ass man myself."

"*That* I have plenty of," she said with a rueful smile.

"Dance?" He held out a hand. "I should have asked before I went all caveman on you."

"Not a Weasel." She smiled genuinely for the first time. "Definitely not a Weasel."

Jordan raised his brows, hand out, waiting. "Not sure what that means, but are you going to give a guy a break here?"

She sighed. "I guess I can." Then she started to turn toward a man sitting by himself at a high top table near them. "Do you want—?"

He snagged her arm, pulled her close. "You're impossible."

"Better you know that now, rather than later." Her lips tipped. "You asked me to give a guy a break."

"*I* was the guy needing a break," he said with a mock glare. Amusement swept through him, especially when she looked up at him with mischief in her gaze.

"Noted," she murmured, allowing him to lead her to the dance floor.

"It's hard work tolerating someone who looks like me, I know," he quipped, wanting to see what she'd say.

"Someone who looks like Thor?" She took a step away and pretended to puke. "Yup. I don't know how I'll stand it."

"Come here, trouble," he said, reeling her in.

And then she was in his arms and it was everything.

The music faded, bar noise became a faint buzz, and it was just the two of them in the universe.

His mind felt quiet for the first time in forever.

Quiet until she gave him sass.

Jordan hated sass. Or *normally* he did. But coming from between Abigail's lips and it had a completely different effect. He liked that she gave him shit. No clue why. Well, none except that fire was infinitely more attractive than soggy dishtowels.

"I keep half expecting you to make a quip about Thor's hammer." One of Abigail's brows lifted, a smile curved the edges of those lush lips. "I hear it's mighty."

"I heard it breaks in the last movie," he joked and when that gorgeous mouth dropped open, he had to laugh. "I didn't say *mine* was broken."

"I'm not interested in yours," she grumbled. "I'm interested in Hemsworth's."

The music changed, a faster song that would make it difficult for them to talk and dance. Jordan snagged her hand before she could slip away. "Another drink?"

She shook her head.

"Food then? This place has good appetizers. The crab cakes are fresh and the artichoke dip is perfectly seasoned." *Come on, O'Keith.* Jordan mentally shook his head, knowing that he sounded like an idiotic Yelp review.

When was the last time he'd stumbled over words with a woman?

Hell, when was the last time he'd actually *talked* to a woman who wasn't a coworker? Or his sister?

Or both, since he actually worked with his sister.

He mentally calculated the hours he'd spent in the office—the *months*—and felt horror course through him. How deprived had his life become if he couldn't remember the last time he'd gotten laid?

Abigail's white teeth bit down on her bottom lip and his cock went rock hard.

That right there was the sign it had been way too long.

He was getting random, uncontrolled boners like a teenage boy.

Yes, it had been harder and harder for him to find the time and energy for sex over the last few years. Especially when every woman who was interested in him was the same.

Plastic. Botox. Extensions. Makeup at the Kardashian level.

Sometimes a man just wanted a real woman.

And Abigail in his arms was that in every sense. Her body actually moved beneath his hands, yielded in a way that made him want to strip her naked and stroke her from head to toe. She didn't wear perfume that masked her scent, clothes that were designed to tempt him.

She was herself.

Which was a thousand times more attractive than a woman who tried too hard.

"Not too hungry?" he asked when she opened her mouth. He could see the refusal on her lips. "We could—"

"No," she said, taking a step back. "No dinner."

His heart clenched with something very much like disappointment. *Damn.* He was really starting to like this woman.

He dropped his hand from hers. "Okay."

"I want dessert." She closed the distance between them,

breasts pressed against his chest. Her mouth was an inch from his skin, her breath hot and damp on his throat.

"At my place," she added, tongue flicking out to graze his skin.

"Oh," he said, gripping her waist to keep her close. *Oh.*

Articulate? No. But, fuck yeah. He could do dessert.

And seconds too.

THREE

Abby

MY PLACE WAS A BLOCK AWAY, a third-floor walk-up
that was perched atop a drug store.

It wasn't much, but it had two bedrooms, a recently remod-
eled kitchen, and only one shared wall. After my last place, it
was practically nirvana.

I'd had the neighbors from hell. On both sides.

In fact, it was as though they'd signed up for a contest to see
who could be the most annoying, disrespectful, and downright
rude.

Late night parties had been only the start.

Things had progressed to growing their own pot plants and
nearly setting the whole building on fire with their heat lamps.
Then fighting over said ownership of the plants in the middle of
the night. Then throwing the plants out of the window when
they couldn't agree.

Onto my car.

And that had just been the neighbor on my left.

The ones on my right were in the Mafia. Or smuggling

illegal ivory. Or hiding a hatcheted up dead guy in the freezer.

So moving had been a priority.

It turned out the move was extremely convenient tonight. Especially considering the hot, hard man pressed so closely behind me I could barely walk.

His arm was snaked around my rib cage, brushing the underside of my breasts, teasing me with every breath I took.

"Just up these stairs," I said, raising my chin in the direction of my apartment.

We walked up the private staircase and paused outside my door. I punched in the code above the handle and said to his questioning look, "I can never find my keys." I turned the knob. "This is easier."

"I like easy."

Like what I was about to be. And with that lovely thought, I started to have doubts.

Jordan turned to close the door, locking the dead bolt with an ominous *click*. This was the moment we'd either find out we didn't mesh in bed or he'd really been after Seraphina and had only settled for a late-night fuck from her pudgy friend as consolation. This was the time he'd—

"Maybe we should have a glass of wine?"

Ask if I wanted wine?

I wrinkled my nose. "Can't stand the stuff."

"Really? How about char—"

I put my hand up to stop the how-about-this-wine-that-is-the-most-spectacular-wine-on-the-planet spiel.

People always wanted to tell me I hadn't found the right variety. That I hadn't expanded my horizons enough.

Couldn't a woman just not like wine?

"I've tried them all." My other palm came up when his mouth opened again. "All. Of. Them."

One side of his mouth tipped up. "All?"

I nodded. "As bad as that is. I know we're basically in wine central, but I just don't like it."

"You're allowed to not like wine."

I snorted. "Not according to some people in this area. You'd think it was a capital offense."

Jordan came close, slipped one hand around my waist, and rested the other on the back of my neck. "It practically is."

"Oh God." I sighed and dropped my head back. "You're one of them too."

Lips on my neck, soft, hot words on my skin. "One of who?"

"One of those crazy winos who waxes poetic about hints of sandalwood and notes of rose."

I gasped when his tongue traced up my throat and paused behind my ear where he stopped and inhaled deeply. "Talk about notes of rose. The scent of your hair is driving me insane. What do you put in it?"

"In . . . it?" I asked, struggling to hold on to the conversation when the man's tongue was running over that sweet spot just below my ear. I barely held back a moan, which was embarrassing enough when he seemed totally unaffected. "Nothing. Just shampoo and conditioner."

"Mmm." He slid his fingers through my hair, up to the tie holding the unruly locks in place. "And I do like wine, but not as much as I like you in this moment."

Gently, he pulled the elastic free and tossed it to the floor.

I barely had a second to worry about it being lost in the black hole that all hair ties seemed to disappear into before his hands found my scalp and began massaging.

If it hadn't felt so good, been so perfectly erotic—my nerve endings on edge, my skin heated, his hard form pressing so tightly to my spine, his erection like granite against my ass—I might have been a little wigged out.

The dude wasn't taking my clothes off. Instead, he was playing with my hair.

But it felt good.

I relaxed against him, jostling his hands loose. Which was fine because those hands had moved from my hair to my body. And that was really, *really* nice too.

"There you are," he murmured. "In the future, just tell me if you want to stop." He tilted my chin back, our faces mismatched as I looked up and he leaned over me to meet my eyes.

Even upside down, he was beautiful.

"You say stop and I'll stop. Yes?"

I nodded. "Yes."

My eyes closed and my head rested against his chest as his palms slipped under my shirt. Goose bumps broke out on my skin and I realized what he'd done.

Calmed me.

Sensed I was nervous and had taken the time to settle the anxiety instead of pushing.

My lips curved.

"Good?" he asked.

"Good," I said, turning in his arms. Blue eyes bored into mine. "You're so pretty," I crooned, reaching up to stroke his cheeks. Stubble bristled my palms as I cupped his face and brought his lips down to mine.

He groaned, hands on my hips, tugging me close, and my confidence lifted. I felt like the woman in the bar again. The one who'd been secure enough to proposition a god.

I touched my tongue to his bottom lip, and he opened his mouth, transforming what I'd thought was already a hot kiss into an inferno and turning my control of the situation into a flash in the pan.

Jordan took over, hands and mouth working my body like an instrument.

Calloused fingertips slid up my ribs, reached around to unhook my bra, and whipped it and my shirt over my head.

"I—"

He paused, eyes molten, breath fast. "Problem?"

"Only that you're still wearing your shirt."

Buttons popped, cotton tore, and then there was only skin.

Tan, hot skin and hard muscles. That mythical eight-pack? I'd seen the unicorn, apparently, because here was one in the flesh.

"I work out"—he dipped his head, took one of my nipples in his mouth, and I moaned—"a lot."

"Mmm," I said, not caring about the words, only wanting him close, to keep his mouth on me. "Are you a personal trainer?"

"Something like that." He paused and an emotion crossed his face, one that disappeared quickly as he switched breasts. Teeth made me jump, the sting soothed by his tongue as one hand came up to tease my other nipple.

My knees buckled.

"I got you," he said, sweeping me up in his arms and dropping me onto the couch.

The leather was cool against my bare skin, but he was shirtless against me. I had plenty to keep me warm.

My hands came up to his shoulders then into the fine hairs at the base of his skull. I loved that spot, loved how it brought him closer, loved how it made him kiss me harder.

His tongue swept along my bottom lip and slipped inside to tangle with mine, his palms gripped my waist tightly. I was on fire, writhing to get closer.

"Easy," he crooned. "I've got you. I've—"

I released his hair and slipped my hands between us, yanking at the button on his slacks, wrenching the zipper down, brushing the massive erection—excuse me, *hammer*—in the process.

Jordan's head plunked onto my chest and he groaned. "Christ, Abby, slow down." He pulled my hands free of his pants, but my work was done. The slacks were out of my way. "It's been a while since I've done this and I want to—"

"Shh," I said. "*I* want to touch."

My fingers slipped into his boxer briefs and he hissed out a breath.

"Too hard?" I asked, my mouth finding one of his nipples and returning his earlier favor.

"No—" He groaned again. "It's too good. You need to—"

"No such thing," I said, stroking him with one hand, while I shoved my leggings down with the other.

I was multi-talented like that.

His fingers slipped between my thighs and it was my turn to gasp. That one touch was liquid lightning. I needed him.

"Abby," he whispered and slipped a finger inside. "Fuck, you're wet."

"I want you," I said. "Now."

"I need to—" He broke off when I wriggled my hips free of his hand and brushed the tip of his erection against my center. "Condom," he gasped.

I'd never had sex without one before, but I was safe. From pregnancy, at least. "I've had an IUD for years," I said, rubbing closer to the heat of him, pressing down on the tip and groaning at the size of him.

Barely an inch in and he was stretching me to capacity.

"And I'm clean," I added, shifting to take him a little deeper.

"Me too, but Abby, it's been awhile. I haven't—"

I didn't care about the rest of his words, instead lurching forward so that he was all the way inside.

"Oh *fuck*," he groaned.

"Oh fuck," I moaned. It was so, so good.

Especially when his leash seemed to snap and he picked me up, keeping himself deep while he swept a hand over my coffee table to clear it.

The remotes went one way, my coasters the other. A paperback landed with a smack against the floor.

He knelt, laying me on the wooden surface and dropping to his knees on one end. My legs wrapped around his hips as he drove into me.

Pleasure rushed through me, rising rapidly. Sweat broke out on my forehead, my muscles locked, and it was right . . . *there*—

"Shit," he said. "*Shit*. I'm sor—" His moan cut off his words, and I barely registered them myself.

What I did register was the thrusts slowing when I needed them to go faster.

I squirmed closer, needing—

"I'm sorry," he said. "It's been a long time."

"I—" My eyes flashed open as he pulled out.

Had he just—?

The throb between my legs was intense. My skin was tight, flushed. My brain was foggy, trying to understand.

"This never happens," he said. "Just give me a second."

"Did you just come?" I blurted, the haze of desire receding as incredulity took over. "*Without me?*"

Fuck if Thor's hammer really wasn't broken.

Jordan scowled. "It's been a long time. I'll take care of you." He hitched his pants up around his hips and reached toward me. "Which way is your bedroom?"

"Down the—"

His phone rang.

I froze. He wasn't going to pick it up. No, he definitely wasn't. Not when I was a twisted pile of need stretched out on a

—really uncomfortable, as it turned out—coffee table. Naked while he was half dressed. Orgasm-free when he was not.

So no, he wouldn't pick up the damn phone.

He wouldn't. He . . . would.

His hands reached to the back of his pants and he snatched up the phone, swiping a finger across the screen.

"What?" he barked, eyes on me. I felt the heat of his stare on my breasts, my lips, my puss—

Maybe this night wouldn't be a total implosion after all.

Then I saw his body change.

Whoever was on the other end said something that made him stiffen and rise to his feet.

Then reach for his shirt. And button it . . . or rather attempt to button it since half of the little disks were scattered on my carpet.

"What the fuck?" I whispered, more to myself than Jordan.

Because Jordan was no longer in the room.

His eyes slipped from me as easily as someone ignores a vagrant on the street. One second to analyze, the next to dismiss.

I propped myself up, wincing when the wood bit into my hip.

I watched Jordan as he walked to the door, spouting terse orders, not sparing a single backward glance for the woman he'd left unsatisfied and naked on the table.

Not another look at me.

The door slammed closed.

FOUR

Abby, Eight Weeks Later

"I'M SEARCHING FOR TREASURE, baby. Can I look around your chest for it?"

My eyes rolled . . . again.

"I need more booze for this," I muttered, bringing my glass of rum and Diet Coke to my lips and taking a sip.

Gross. And I didn't just mean the bad pickup line. My drink tasted horrible. It was probably the absence of the calorie-laden Coke. Sugar helped the alcohol go down easier. But my pants were a little tight and that meant that I needed to cut back on life's extras until my skinny jeans stopped giving me a muffin top.

With a sigh, I took another sip and almost gagged.

Apparently, my taste buds weren't feeling the combination.

Whatever. I was adult enough to not force myself to choke down something that tasted horrible. I plunked the glass on the bar top and pushed it away, pulling my phone out of my purse with my other hand.

"We should go," Seraphina said. "I don't know why we even bothered."

"It was because we got through lunch the other day without interruption," I said, lips curving at her pained expression. "Of course, we were probably naïve not to realize it was because the place was packed with women."

The Tea House was one of our favorite places and not just because they served tea and crumpets—actual crumpets!—but because it was small and cozy and made us feel as though we'd stumbled into a historical novel.

The clientele was also not particularly masculine.

"It's lunchtime now," she whispered. "Don't these jerks have to work?"

"Apparently not," I whispered back as another came up to the bar and leaned close to my friend.

Who leaned away so quickly that she nearly knocked me off my stool.

"You like onions, huh?" Seraphina asked, and I wrinkled my nose.

"Who doesn't?" the man replied back, as much oil coating his words as coated his head. "But what I'm really liking is that shirt."

His eyes drifted down and stuck and I had the overwhelming urge to gag. Not just from his tone and his near orgasm over a flipping T-shirt. But because the rancid onion smell had hit my nostrils.

I stood, clamping a hand over my mouth. "I'm going to the bathroom."

"As soon as you get back, let's go." She glanced at the bartender who all but sprinted over. "I'll settle our tab."

I nodded, leaving my palm where it was, and rushed to the hallway leading to the toilets.

My stomach roiled and I wondered if I was getting sick. The

last time I felt like this—weak, nauseous, sweaty—I'd had the flu. Except then—

"*Oof!*" My hand compressed painfully against my jaw as I collided with a wall.

Or rather, what felt like a wall.

Instead, it was male and very hard and . . . my gut contracted—

Extremely Thor-like.

What. The. Fuck.

My insides heaved and I shoved at Jordan's hands, which had come up to steady me.

"Easy now," he said, and his voice slid over me in the same way as that night eight weeks before.

Jesus Christ, I thought as I shivered in anticipation. *What was wrong with me?*

"Abigail?"

I dropped my hand from my mouth, stomach abruptly settling as I glared at him. "Is that a question?" I asked caustically and yanked myself out of his grip. "Or do you struggle to remember the names of all the girls you screw and leave wanting?"

"I—"

I leaned in and hissed, "I had to get myself off after you used me like a sex toy to get your jollies and then strolled out the door."

"Jollies?" His lips quirked, and I saw red.

"Yes, *jollies.*" My hands found my hips and though I was slightly horrified by what I was saying, I pressed on. He'd had sex with me and left without a goodbye. "You left me naked on my coffee table."

I hadn't heard from him for eight weeks and he was here in the bar saying my name like a question?

Yeah, no.

He knew where I lived, for fuck's sake. Maybe a little pop by with a reciprocal orgasm could have been provided?

Just a thought.

"You ruined what I'd hoped was going to be the best sex of my life and . . . *and* you broke my favorite coffee mug."

He crossed his arms when I paused, chest heaving. "You done?"

I blew out a sigh and started to push past him. "Yeah. I'm beyond done."

Jordan waited until my back was to him before he bent and whispered in my ear, "I didn't want to leave."

"Could have fooled me." I wrinkled my nose when a scent hit me and it wasn't pleasant. Almost sour, it sent my stomach twisting again.

"I had a very important work call I needed to take."

"Now that," I said, "I read loud and clear."

"Abby." He took my arm, spun me to face him.

I would have been irritated by the manhandling if the smell hadn't been so horrible and all-encompassing.

What *was* that?

My brain was processing it as rotting garbage, spoiled milk, and onion breath all wrapped up in one disgusting package.

I gagged, eyes searching the hall for the source of the scent.

I couldn't find anything.

Except for Jordan.

"It's *you*."

My stomach heaved and I shoved away from him, running for the women's bathroom.

"What's me? Abby?" He grabbed my arm again, and I jerked free, pushing into the single stall. I didn't have time to worry about the door closing, let alone locking, barely making it to the toilet as I lost my breakfast.

Tears streamed down my cheeks, my throat burned, and the

nausea didn't abate as my body pitched a proverbial fit for several long minutes.

Finally, when it seemed like I was done, I leaned back on my heels, tilted my head toward the ceiling, and reached blindly for the handle to flush the toilet.

Warm fingers beat me, sending the mess down the drain. My eyes flashed open and, of course, Jordan was there. Unlike me, he'd crouched down, sparing his impeccable suit from the dirty bar tile.

My jeans were probably ruined.

"Here," he said and handed me a damp paper towel.

I took it, turning my head away as I wiped my eyes then the corners of my lips. I pushed to my feet, needing to rinse my mouth out in the sink.

"You okay?"

I spit and took another mouthful from the faucet to swish around. No, I definitely wasn't okay. I'd just puked in front of the hottest man I'd ever seen, the same one who'd seen me naked, who'd been having sex with me, and still decided that his work call was more important than me finishing.

"I'm fine."

Turning, I started for the door, only to have Jordan stop me again.

"I'm sorry about that night."

I snorted. "Me too."

"I didn't want to leave."

With a shrug, I shook his hand loose and headed for the door. "Go away, Jordan."

"I *had* to go."

"Reading that loud and clear." I yanked the handle and entered the hall.

Jordan stepped in front of me and bent down so that his face was near mine again.

That bitter smell curled around my nostrils again, seeping in and making my gut roil.

"Back up," I snapped. "You smell horrible."

His mouth dropped open. "I *what?*"

"You. Smell. Horrible."

He lifted one lapel of his suit jacket, tilting his head down and sniffing. "I smell fine."

I clapped a hand to my nose and took a step back, my words slightly nasally when I said, "If you say so."

He inhaled on the other side. "Nothing. Just my deodorant." He looked up at me. "I wanted to apologize for that night. I was off my game and in the middle of a huge merger. I had no business going home with anyone at that time." His eyes locked with mine. "It wasn't my intention to leave you . . ."

"Wanting?"

A flash of something crossed his expression. Heat? Frustration? Regret?

Since I'd been intimately familiar with those emotions over the last few months, I smirked. Then I turned and walked away.

My exit was almost good enough to make me forget that I'd tossed my cookies in front of him.

Almost.

Because Jordan was still the most gorgeous man I'd ever seen.

FIVE

Jordan

JORDAN WATCHED Abigail's ass as she walked away from him. God, it was a good ass. Two perfectly plump handfuls he'd spent the last eight weeks dreaming about.

And he was finally done with the buyout.

Finally ready to spend the foreseeable future on a private stretch of beach in the Caribbean.

A stretch that he now owned.

His private jet was fueled, the pilot on standby.

So why wasn't he already in the air?

Unfinished business.

With the curvy brunette who was moving further out of reach by the moment.

He trailed her across the bar to the blond model-type, Suzette or Sandy or some S-name. Heads dipped together and twin glares were thrown his way.

That might have made him smile. If he weren't so desperate to improve Abigail's impression of him.

Not just in the bedroom, either. Love them and leave them

wasn't his style. Jordan was more of a serial monogamist. And since he hadn't found a woman in a long time who would tolerate his long work hours, frequently broken dates, not to mention panicked phone calls from his staff at all hours of the day, it had been a long time since he'd had an orgasm that came courtesy of a member of the opposite sex.

Aside from Palm-ela, that was.

Inwardly snorting at his own awful joke, he plastered on a confident smile, and approached the girls.

"Ladies, can I buy you another round? Maybe some food?" The mention of food made Abby's face go pale and he gritted his teeth. Of course she wouldn't want food. She'd just been heaving up breakfast in the bathroom.

"No food," he said quickly.

"Stop mentioning food," Abigail ground out, one hand coming to her stomach, the other to her mouth.

"Abs?" the S-friend asked. "Are you okay?"

"I'm fine," she said. "Just not feeling good."

"Well our tab is paid, so we can go."

Jordan stood like a useless floor lamp shoved into a corner as he watched the girls talk.

He wasn't in the habit of being ignored and though it wasn't something he enjoyed admitting, he didn't like it one bit.

He was important.

Correction, he *used* to be important.

Now he was just an out-of-work inventor. Granted, one with a couple of billion in the bank, but still, he was at loose ends.

Beach ends, he reminded himself.

"I'm just going to head home," Abigail was saying. "Go to bed early and hope that this thing blows over quickly."

"Okay, love. Want me to walk with you?"

Abby opened her mouth but the sound of a cell phone ringing stoppered any words that might have emerged.

Jordan reached for his cell then remembered he didn't have one any longer.

It was relief that coursed through him, not a pang for the job, and certainly not a desire to go back to somewhere he was needed.

His—*the*—company was in good hands. He was going back to his roots. His wallet was just a little thicker.

"Go, Seraphina" Abby whispered, gesturing to the bar's entrance as her friend picked up the call. "I'm fine."

"Talk to you later," Seraphina mouthed before taking off.

"Okay," Abby murmured and tucked her purse over her shoulder. She turned for the door without a glance back at him.

Which was fine.

Because Jordan knew where she lived.

He let Abigail leave, giving her a thirty-second head start before following her.

She was barely a block away and he used his long legs to his advantage, catching up to her in hardly any time at all.

Shortening his stride to match hers, he didn't say anything as he walked next to her.

Her breath caught when she peeked up at him, but the verbal litany he'd expected to greet him didn't come.

Hazel eyes stayed forward, ignoring him.

Ah. They'd progressed to the silent treatment.

He could work with that.

Keeping pace, he stayed at her side as they walked to her apartment.

Patience was his strong suit, and he'd spent every spare moment of the last two months imagining all the ways he was going to make up that night to her.

It hadn't been until hours after the call that he'd realized exactly what he'd done to her. When Abby had said he'd used her like a sex toy, she'd been right.

He'd acted like a premature teenager and then hadn't even bothered to explain or make it up to her. Yes, that phone call had put his business deal on the razor's edge of falling through the cracks and almost destroyed every single thing he'd been working toward for years.

But he wasn't a user.

That was his father's job.

So now that the deal was tied up in a neat little package and the checks had cleared, he was going to explain and, if she let him, make it up to her.

"I shouldn't have left without a goodbye."

Abigail's feet stuttered, missing a step before her chin came up and her lips pressed into a firm line.

Ruby red and plump, that mouth sent heat right through him.

He wanted to kiss her. He wanted to *talk* to her.

Which should have sent him running.

Instead, he was right there next to her.

"I was in the process of selling my business and the call I received . . . well, it jeopardized everything I'd been working for."

Jordan stopped talking and waited for her to say something.

She didn't.

He sighed. He might need more than patience for another shot with this one.

"I—"

"Will you just shut up?" she snapped.

He paused, rocking back on his heels as she stormed on and for the first time, he wondered if he'd been daydreaming about the wrong woman all these weeks. Yes, she was beautiful, but maybe she wasn't what he remembered.

Fiery yet tempered with vulnerability. Kindness for her friend. Self-deprecating and funny.

Maybe she was just mean.

And he had spent too long with mean to take up with it again.

Jordan hesitated, feet pointed back toward the bar and the lot his car was parked in. Maybe instead of trying to make it up to her, he'd drive to the airport and hit his private stretch of oceanfront.

Then Abby began running.

"Wh—"

They were less than a block from her apartment and she was sprinting for it like the hounds of hell were after her.

He knew he hadn't been that bad in bed. Okay, on the *table*. Right?

But it was her posture that finally snapped him out of his stupor. She was bent at the waist, hand across her stomach, head tilted down, and she was barely watching where she was going.

Thankfully, the sidewalks weren't crowded but she wasn't looking. She could knock over a little old lady, crash into a street sign. Hell, she could miss the edge of the sidewalk and get hit by a car.

Which was the thought that finally propelled him forward.

He ran toward her, catching her arm and tugging her away from a trash can. "Careful, you almost hit—"

"I *need* that," she groaned, ripping free and whipping back to the receptacle.

And for the second time in less than an hour, Jordan watched Abby toss her cookies.

Funny how the sight would typically make him run, but with Abby, he stayed beside her.

Albeit, he still had no idea what he should be doing.

Holding back her hair? Rubbing her shoulders?

She didn't seem to like it when he touched her, so he opted for searching his pockets for a tissue and shifting from foot to foot.

This round didn't last as long as the first. Thankfully. For her. Because he definitely wasn't feeling relief at not having to find something else to keep himself occupied while she was feeling horrible.

"I'm sorry," he said.

She rested her head against the metal rim of the garbage bin. "Me too."

They stood like that for a few moments, awkward and unmoving. He wanted to ask if he could help, but he sensed that she was trying to figure out if she was done.

Finally, she raised her head and winced. "I need to get home."

"I'll help you."

Hazel eyes skewered him. "Help only. Promise," he added when her glare didn't relax.

"Okay, fine." She wrinkled her nose. "I meant, thank you. Yes, I'm still mad at you, but I'm not a total troll and you didn't leave me heaving my guts up on the side of the road, so . . ."

"That counts as something?" He grinned at her.

She huffed out a breath. "A small something."

"Progress. Here." He took her purse from where it had slipped down to her elbow. "Let me carry that for you."

"Thanks," she murmured then squinted up at her building and the three flights of stairs to her apartment. "Why did I like this walk-up so much?"

"Exercise?" he joked as she headed for the building.

"Pish, exercise is overrated. I'd give anything for an elevator right about now."

He touched her arm. "I can carry you."

"I'm fine."

Since she didn't exactly *look* fine, Jordan stayed close. Her skin was waxy and pale. Even her lips weren't as rosy as they'd been minutes before.

He slipped an arm around her waist, shushing her when she started to pull free.

"Just let me help you," he said. "You've still got two flights to go."

She groaned. "I thought I was almost there."

"Forget this," he said and swept a hand under her knees, pulling her up into his arms.

It was a good thing he chose that moment to ignore her wishes because the second she was against his chest, Abigail's eyes rolled back and her entire body went limp.

He cradled her close, spent a half second enjoying the weight of her against him before Jordan realized that he held an unconscious woman in his arms.

He climbed the last two flights of stairs in rapid time then carefully laid Abby against her door as he searched her bag for the keys to her apartment. She'd put in a code on the keypad that night, but he hadn't seen it, and after a few minutes of searching the black hole that was her purse, he dumped the entire contents on the ground next to her.

Nothing.

Or, well, no keys.

There were about a million other articles—junk—in the feminine depths. But no keys.

Shit.

He reached a hand into his pocket and remembered all at once he didn't have a phone.

Which had been a tactical decision at the time. To be unreachable.

To be free.

Jordan realized that had been a really fucking stupid idea.

He'd figured that he could always use someone else's phone if it came down to it. But the only other person around at the moment was unconscious, so that plan was in the crapper.

Except, she *had* a phone.

He'd seen it in the mess on the ground. Shoving tampons and receipts to the side, he unearthed the smartphone and pressed the home button.

Locked.

He cursed. Of course it was locked, and he knew the PIN to Abby's phone as readily as he knew the code to her apartment.

Abby moaned, and he cupped her cheek.

Maybe she was coming around and could unlock the phone herself. Then he could call someone. But after a long moment of him waiting for signs of consciousness and her not waking up, Jordan recognized that he was well and truly fucked.

He dropped his hands from her face and pressed his fingers to her pulse point at her wrist.

Steady.

So she'd wake up. Right?

But now it had been longer than he was comfortable with. Her hands were like ice, and she was so, so pale.

Damn. He had to do something.

When it occurred to him, he realized he was an idiot.

Jordan picked up her hand, pressed her right thumb to the home button.

It worked. The screen unlocked and he hurriedly keyed in 9-1-1.

"I need an ambulance."

SIX

Abby

I WAS FREEZING. My stomach felt as though it had gone five rounds with the Tilt-A-Whirl.

With a groan, I peeled back my eyelids and winced against the bright lights.

Where the hell was I?

Last I remembered, I'd been puking into another trash can. In front of—and thank you, universe, for that one—Jordan. For the second time.

Awesome. Lovely. The perfect ending to what had amounted to a hellish last two months for me.

"You're awake."

I carefully turned my head to the side and, of course, Jordan was there, looking gorgeous in his suit. It fit his body like a second skin, and *my* body remembered the feel of all that glorious hardness in minute, extremely descriptive detail.

The heat of him. The prickle of stubble against my throat. The way his abs had felt like granite. The press of his hipbones to mine. Hard to soft. Hot to warm. Spicy. Masculine—

Not. Mine.

"I'm awake," I agreed and closed my eyes, shifting my head back to the center of my pillow.

"You passed out," he said.

The lights were uncomfortably bright through my lids, so I tilted my head again. Away from Jordan.

"Yeah," I said. "I'm getting that."

"You scared me."

The words made me jump, not only because they surprised the hell out of me, but also because they came from approximately eight inches away from my face.

I hadn't heard him move, but he was there. Crouched next to the bed and right in my face.

"I'm sorry." And I was. "Thanks for not leaving me."

Jordan's brows pulled down. "Why would I have left you?"

"Um, because I was mean to you and puking uncontrollably."

He snorted. "Fair point. But I don't think you were feeling like yourself."

Now wasn't that the truth? I'd been feeling off for a couple of weeks but had chalked it up to my hypoglycemia. Which basically meant that my body didn't process insulin correctly and my blood sugar dropped unpredictably. But other than small, frequent meals and sometimes getting a little dizzy, it hadn't affected my life all that much.

Trust it to make me pass out for the first time in my life in front of a god.

Now *that* fit in with how things had been going as of late.

"My assistant couldn't find your insurance card."

I blinked, eyes flying to his. There was something in his expression . . . calculating? Careful?

Whatever it was, I didn't like it.

"It's in my apartment." I sighed. "I was using it to apply for new insurance. I was laid off this week."

He grimaced. "I'm sorry."

"Yeah. Me too." My job gone in the span of fifteen minutes. And I couldn't even say it was because I'd screwed up or the owners had been unfair.

Frank and Susan deserved their retirement. Except, I'd all but run their graphic design business for the last few years. It had become my baby, and now it was gone.

"My bosses decided they needed to simplify their life, sold the business, and bought a giant RV." I shrugged. "At least they left me a nice severance package. I'm good for a bit."

Not that I knew what I wanted to do with my life. Did I want to spend the rest of it designing websites and logos?

No, I didn't think so.

But I also didn't have a reasonable source of income.

And a girl needed money to survive.

"That's good," Jordan said.

I pushed all thoughts of my former job out of my head and focused on my immediate surroundings. Which I probably should have done the moment I woke, but there you go. My brain didn't always work in a straightforward, A to B, important to least important way.

Sometimes I got stuck on insignificant details and veered off course.

Sometimes I fussed with the placement of one letter for hours, so focused on that one small point that I forgot about the big picture.

"How'd I get here?"

"An ambulance."

"*What?*" I guess I figured he'd driven me, because damn, being transported to the hospital in an ambulance for my hypo-glycemia was going to be expensive.

Shit.

Jordan's lips pressed together. "You wouldn't wake up, and I couldn't get into your apartment. I was worried."

"I'm sorry. I'm just—" I shook my head. "Nothing like this has ever happened to me before. Aside from a lot of tests when I was younger"—I explained my hypoglycemia and what it meant —"I've never even been in the hospital."

He nodded, looking thoughtful. "The doctor said something about your blood sugar being off."

"Dang," I said. "I—"

A warm hand laced with mine. "Hey, it's okay. The doctors will get you sorted out and you'll be on your way."

My nose wrinkled as the smell of Jordan—was it his deodorant? It almost had a spicy scent, like men's grooming products— hit my nose again. In a second, I went from feeling a little weak but mostly fine, to my stomach tying itself in knots.

"Let go." I pulled my hand free, scooted back on the bed. "Stay there," I said when he leaned in, face concerned.

"What is it?"

I put a palm up. "That smell. You." I tried to breathe through my mouth as saliva pooled around my tongue. "Your . . . deodorant."

Don't puke. No puking allowed—

I gagged.

Jordan backed up.

"I can't with the smell. It's horrible. It's going to make me pu—"

He snagged a trash can from near the door and extended it toward me. "I don't understand why the smell of my deodorant is making you sick—"

The door opened and a doctor filled the threshold, taking in the garbage bin on the bed, my hand over my mouth, and Jordan pressed into the corner.

"Stomach still touchy, huh?" The doctor, a middle-aged man in blue scrubs and a white coat, with gray-blond hair neatly combed, pushed through the door. He used his palm to press some sanitizer from the container mounted on the wall and rubbed it between his hands.

I nodded. "Yes, unfortunately." Though the roiling was subsiding with Jordan out of nose-reach.

"I'm Dr. Williams." He crossed to the computer and typed a few keys before scrolling through several screens. "I think I have the answer to that."

"My hypoglycemia?"

Dr. Williams turned and came close to the bed. "Your hypoglycemia was almost certainly the reason for the fainting. Your stomach upset is for a completely different reason, I suspect."

I frowned.

"When was the date of your last period?"

I pressed back into the bed. "I've had an IUD for years. I hardly ever get periods anymore. It's been months."

Dr. Williams sighed. "Well, here's the thing. We drew your blood"—he nodded at the bandage at my elbow—"and that sample says you're pregnant."

My entire body went numb. That couldn't be right. I hadn't—

I couldn't—

"In fact, your HCG levels say you're about eight weeks pregnant."

I felt Jordan move in the corner, but I couldn't tear my eyes away from the doctor.

"But I have an IUD."

"Unfortunately, no method of birth control is one hundred percent effective." He gave me a sympathetic look. "In fact, my youngest daughter is the byproduct of a failed IUD."

This couldn't actually be happening.

Not now. Not with my job imploding. Not with my dad deciding—

A hand touched mine and I opened my eyes to find Dr. Williams staring down at me, dark eyes kind. "You'll be okay. The OB will be down in a few minutes to check on you and then you can get out of here. You'll need to make some follow up appointments to ensure you and the baby stay healthy, all right?"

"All right." I gripped the sheets tightly as he logged out of the computer and left the room. The cotton was cool against my clammy hands, but it was more than that. Something concrete to hold on to when the rest of the world was falling apart.

I was ignoring the fact that I was going to have to let go at some point.

Pregnant.

How in the hell was I pregnant?

"Goodbye, Abigail. Take care." And with a small smile, Dr. Williams was gone.

I stared at the ceiling for a few minutes before I frowned and glanced around the room.

Jordan was gone.

How typical.

SEVEN

Abby

"SO YOUR PRESCRIPTIONS should be ready by the time you're out of here, and you'll need to follow up with me in two weeks," Dr. Stephens said.

She was a young blond woman with a perky ponytail and honey-colored eyes. Her gaze was warm and her demeanor straightforward.

I liked her. Despite where her hands were.

"There," she said after a moment and turned the ultrasound machine so that I could see the black and white picture.

My heart stuttered, and I ignored the uncompromising wand between my legs for the first time since it had made its appearance. "Is that—?"

"Your baby?" Dr. Stephens hit a button on the machine, printing out the image. "Yes. Or maybe I should say, there's your raspberry since your little one is just about the size of one of those berries."

"Really?" I asked, my hand coming to my belly.

"Really," the doctor said. "And this here. The fluttering?"

I nodded.

"That's the baby's heartbeat. Which looks nice and strong."

Relief coursed through me. I hadn't even realized I'd been tense, but everything that was happening seemed so fragile. So small.

A raspberry.

I could crush it with barely a thought. An hour ago, I'd thought I was coming down with the flu, and now I had a baby inside me.

Evidence that I could see on the ultrasound, could *hear* on the ultrasound—my baby's heartbeat whooshing away.

And instead of panicking, instead of freaking out, I just felt relief that he or she was okay.

That I hadn't screwed up *this* part of my life.

Not yet anyway.

"So everything looks great," Dr. Stephens said and slid the wand free.

I wrinkled my nose at the feeling of lubricant between my thighs. It was cold and sticky. Gross.

"Because of your health history, I'll want to keep a closer eye on you than my typical patients." Her ponytail bounced as she peeled off her gloves. "That is, if you want to continue your care with me. You can easily see your normal gynecologist for the duration of your pregnancy."

"I don't actually have a gynecologist."

"Good. I'll take you." White teeth flashed before Dr. Stephens frowned. "When was your last pap smear?"

"Uhh." I bit my lip. "Maybe five, six years ago? I'm not sure."

"Well, that won't do. Let me see if I can find anything on your chart. Was it in this hospital?"

"Yes." I gave her my former doctor's name and saw her nose wrinkle. "Yeah," I said, "he wasn't exactly my favorite."

"Honestly?" Honey eyes met mine. "He wasn't my favorite either. Let's see." She scrolled down several screens on the computer. "Ah. There it is. Seven years ago."

"Oh. Is that—?"

"Don't worry, we'll get you caught up." She smiled. "And it's completely safe to do during pregnancy. That way we'll tick it off the list while I have you here and your results should be in by the next time you're in the office." She pulled out a phone from her pocket. "Let me just find out if there are any kits handy. Hang tight."

The nurse came in barely a minute later, a sealed pack in her hand. Dr. Stephens opened it, arranged it on a tray, and put on a pair of gloves.

"Ready?"

"Joy," I muttered, sliding back down the table to put my feet in the stirrups.

I was in this joyful position, speculum inserted, when the door opened.

At first, I thought it was the nurse and didn't take my eyes from the ceiling.

"Almost done," Dr. Stephens said.

The crash was what made me look.

Jordan had slammed into the tray and was facing the wall.

Jesus Christ.

"I'm sorry," he said to the wallpaper. "I should have knocked. I—"

"Done," the doctor said, covering me as she pulled off her gloves and spun her stool around. "You must be Dad."

"Jordan." He carefully turned, eyes flicking in my direction for a heartbeat before his shoulders visibly relaxed. "I'm Abby's friend."

"Dr. Stephens." She tossed her gloves into the trash and extended a hand before tilting her head in my direction. "Take care of this one, okay?" To me, she said, "Two weeks. I've put the office number on your discharge instructions, so get that appointment on the calendar."

"I will," I said. "Thank you."

With a wave, she left the room.

And cue silence . . . of the awkward variety.

I forced a laugh, crinkling the edges of the paper drape covering my lady business from the rest of the world. "Just when you thought you couldn't see more of me . . ."

I went for a joke because that was all I had.

I mean, really, what could I say? "Here's an even more up-close image of the female parts that couldn't keep you interested. Just what you've always wanted!"

Humor was all I had. Well, that and crying, and I decided that I wasn't quite up to crying in front of Jordan.

Not after our night together.

Tears, panic, and a mental breakdown could come when I was tucked into bed, my softest blanket pulled to my chin, and a worn paperback in one hand.

"What was that doctor doing to you?" Jordan shuddered instead of addressing my lousy joke. "It was like you had a drone up your—"

He broke off, wincing at the same time his cheeks went bright red.

"I'm sorry, I didn't mean it that way." He blew out a breath. "I just mean that it looked uncomfortable, and I wasn't sure if you'd need help and . . ."

"That," I said, deciding to throw him a bone, "was a Pap smear. A lovely procedure where they scrape cells from the surface of a woman's cervix to check for abnormalities. It's uncomfortable, but necessary."

"Was it safe?" he asked. "For the—um . . . for the baby?"

I nodded. "Typical prenatal procedure, I was told." I hesitated for a moment before deciding to press on anyway. "Why are you here?" I put a hand up. "I didn't mean that the way it sounded, just that you heard pregnancy and disappeared. I didn't exactly expect a return trip."

Jordan crossed the room, pausing near my bedside, and I realized that his hair was wet.

"Did you shower?" I asked, incredulous.

He shrugged. "I smelled bad, apparently. I asked Dr. Williams if I could use the physician lounge and he kindly agreed." His smile made my stomach twist, but not in the I'm-going-to-puke way for a change. It looped, knotted itself up in a this-guy-is-the-most-beautiful-specimen-of-manhood-I've-ever-seen, and that bubbly, wiggly feeling actually felt kind of nice.

"Wow," I said and not just because of the wiggly feeling. That he'd showered was perhaps the single most thoughtful thing a member of the opposite sex had ever done for me.

My father included.

"Go on." Jordan lifted an arm, distracting me from the melancholy about my dad and drawing my focus back to him. All things considered, eyeing Jordan's man-meat wasn't exactly a tough job. "Freshly cleaned with unscented soap," he announced. "Your nose should be safe from me."

I gave a cautious sniff and was relieved when my stomach stayed calm.

"Good?"

I inhaled deeper, felt nothing more than a fluttering that had absolutely nothing to do with nausea. "Good."

He smiled and it made my heart skip a beat.

"So," I said, tugging the sheet more fully over my legs, "are we going to talk about this?"

One brow lifted. "About what? The fact that women are way tougher than men could ever hope to be? Or the other thing?"

I bit my lip. "The other thing."

"Want to maybe wait until you're fully clothed for that one?"

Good point.

"I guess. It's just—"

"I know I haven't exactly given you a reason to trust me, but I take care of my responsibilities."

The words might have meant more if I hadn't heard them before, from a man I'd trusted my entire life.

"Okay," I said.

"What is it?" Fingers laced with mine.

I forced a smile. "Let's see, we've danced in a bar, had a one night stand, and a hospital visit, and we haven't even had a first date. Is there anything else on the daytime soap circuit we've missed?"

Jordan laughed. "I don't think so."

"Then let's table all the discussions until I'm no longer bottomless, okay?"

"I can do that." He paused, considering. "So what kind of TV shows do you like?"

"Uh. Are we really doing this?"

"Doing what?"

"The getting to know each other spiel? You've seen my insides."

He fixed me with a look. "I've also seen you naked and know what you sound like when you moan. Though"—his expression went rueful—"not what you sound like when you come. I'd been heading to your apartment, intending to wait around for you. Intending to make that particular part of our evening together up to you, when I saw you go into the bar."

"You saw me?"

"I did." Jordan rubbed a hand against his chin and the sound of his stubble rubbing against his palm raised the hairs on my nape. I remembered the feel of it on my throat, my breasts.

It had all been so good, until it hadn't been. "You wanted to make it up to me?"

"I did," he said again.

"But—" I shook my head.

"That doesn't fit into the image of the asshole who strode out of your apartment without a second glance?"

"Not really, no."

"Well, it doesn't fit into my image of myself either," he said.

Damn.

I'd been so prepared to hate Jordan after our night together, and he was making it really hard to hang onto those feelings.

"So I think it might be best to table all serious discussion and focus on getting to know each other a little better." He squeezed my fingers. "What do you think?"

"I think that's a brilliant idea."

EIGHT

Jordan

JORDAN STOOD NEXT TO ABIGAIL, prepared to catch her if they had a repeat of their last experience on her stairs.

She squinted up at him, rolled her eyes. "I'm fine, you know. Now that I know what's going on with my blood sugar, I'll just be a little more careful about eating."

"Okay," he said, not disagreeing with her, but also not moving from his position behind her. So what if his arms were out and ready to catch?

Abby snorted. "Men are impossible."

"One might make a case—"

"Shh," she said. "I'd stop right there, if I were you."

"Oh?" he asked, all innocence. "So I shouldn't say that women are impossible too?"

"Definitely not," she said, then laughed. "Even if it is very true."

They reached the final few steps and approached her apartment door. Jordan thought she was beautiful in the evening light. The sun made all the different shades in her hair stand out. He wanted to study it, search out each individual color.

He also had entirely too much time on his hands now that he'd sold the business.

Abby put in the code on the keypad, and he did a very good job of pretending not to watch, all while memorizing the four-digit password.

She opened the door then rotated so she was facing him, blocking the entrance to her apartment. "You don't have to come in."

He tilted his head to the side. "Do you want me to leave?"

"Honestly?" she asked.

He nodded despite knowing that she was about to give him his walking papers.

"No."

The word made him rock back on his heels. "Really?"

She huffed and turned her back on him, tossing over her shoulder as she walked inside, "Don't make me regret being honest. Close the door," she added when he stood frozen. "You can pick which side of it you want to be on."

"Smartass."

"You know it." But she blew out a breath when he'd closed and locked the door. "I'm sorry. You've been nothing but nice and patient today."

"Why do I feel there should be an emphasis on *today*?"

"It's not you—" She shook her head. "Not entirely you, anyway. I've had a shitty couple of weeks and this . . ." Her chin dropped to her chest and she sighed deeply. "What the fuck am I going to do with a baby?"

Jordan felt his heart skip a beat. "So you're going to have it?"

If there were wrong words to say, those were the ones.

"It?" Her eyes closed. She sighed and lifted her gaze to mine. "It." Any warmth in her expression had vanished.

"I didn't—"

She walked to the door, opened it. "Out. Don't worry, I won't bother you with *it*."

"Abby." He crossed to her. "That's not what I meant. I didn't want to pressure—"

"*Get out.*"

"I'm not—"

"Get out!" she yelled, tears forming in the corners of her eyes, and just that quickly Jordan snapped.

Crying on cue. Throwing temper tantrums. Manipulating the facts to get something from him.

He'd seen this all before. He'd been through this too many times to count.

He'd just thought that Abby might have been different.

He should have known better.

"Is it even mine?" he hissed, eyeing the worn furniture, the small space. It had seemed cozy and warm all those weeks before. Now he saw it for what it really was.

A play for more.

Abigail gasped. "You—you fucking jerk."

"Now you don't have a job? Oh, and no insurance, too?" He laughed, and if it was bitter, it was because he'd been through this dog and pony show before. He'd seen his father deal with it, had been a victim of the scheme himself.

Lying about being on birth control.

How could he have been so fucking stupid?

His father had fallen for that trick on more than one occasion.

And now, apparently so had he.

Or maybe—

"Are you even pregnant?"

Her jaw dropped open, right on cue. The perfect actress. "You saw—"

"How much did you pay them? God, you had me fooled." He shook his head, forcing away his blip of regret when hurt slid across her face. This was all an act.

And not even a very good one.

"When did you find out I'd sold InDTech? That my bank account is overflowing?"

That's what she wanted. To pretend to be wholesome as she weaseled her way in.

He pulled out his wallet. Opened the leather case.

"You're unbelievable. I don't want anything from you," she snapped. "Except—" Her breath hitched when he extracted a wad of bills and thrust them into her hands.

She fumbled to take the pile, and his anger was confirmed.

"Except money," he spat.

Abigail carefully stacked the hundreds, putting them into a neat pile that she then lifted up to him. "Nothing," she said softly. "Except for you to get the hell out of my apartment, and never bother me again."

"I should have figured that wasn't enough for you." He shook his head and walked over the threshold. "Consider it a down payment for carrying my baby."

The door slammed closed, barely missing his head.

NINE

Abby

I SANK to the hardwood floor in a daze.

What the hell had just happened?

One second Jordan had been sweet, attentive even, the next he was a raging asshole.

Dr. Jekyll, Mr. Hyde, much?

Or maybe it was more Banner-Hulk, since my insides felt smashed to pieces.

Pregnant. I was pregnant, and the father thought I was trying to trap him.

I'd barely had an hour to come to grips with the fact that *a tiny person was growing inside me* and my baby daddy—who I barely knew—had accused me of being a gold digger.

What level of fucked up was that?

If he only knew who my father was, that notion would be laughable.

"Too bad laughter isn't high on my emotions right about now." I pushed to my feet and when I felt a little dizzy, I forced myself into the kitchen for a snack.

I'd grown up with nannies, a private chef, tutors galore. I'd had a designer wardrobe and any toy I'd ever expressed half an interest in.

But none of that had brought me happiness.

Or parents who wanted to be in my life.

I had a trust fund that ended in a line of zeroes longer than my arm. But I didn't touch the money. I didn't have to.

I made my own way.

And if it was a little—okay, a *hell* of a lot—leaner than my childhood, then that was just fine with me.

I had Seraphina and my other friends. I had my job . . . well, I used to have my job. I had my books, and I had rum and Coke.

Which I couldn't have right now.

I sighed.

"Well, baby," I said, and cupped my stomach, wondering if the little raspberry could hear me, "you've made me puke more times today than I've done in the last decade, you've taken my rum and Coke, and made me expose my lady bits to the world for what I suspect is not the last time. What do you say we take it to the bedroom for an early bedtime?"

I could really use a book, a bath, and cuddly pajamas.

Everything else could hold until the morning.

"HE SAID *WHAT* TO YOU?" Seraphina all but shrieked into the phone the next morning. I hadn't wanted to ruin my friend's day like Jordan and the pesky hospital visit had ruined mine, so I'd called her as she drove to work the following day.

I winced and held my cell away from my ear. "I know. It was pretty awful."

"Who in their right mind would think *you* would be a gold digger?" she declared. "He's a moron."

"Well, *that's* obvious," I muttered, switching her to speakerphone as I pulled out my laptop. "All of that drama aside, I guess the question really is what I should do now."

"You need a job."

I nodded, though she couldn't see me. "With good health insurance."

"You know." Her voice was careful. "I'm sure your dad's company could use a graphic designer."

"We've been through this before." I sighed. "I don't want to be that person. And if my dad truly wanted me he would ask."

"He *did* ask."

"No, he offered me a fluff position with no real responsibility," I reminded her. "I'm happy to work my way through the ranks, but I refuse to be a puppet that no one respects. Plus, I don't think after our last interactions I'll be ready to work for him in any real capacity for a good long time."

My father wanted me to work for him. *That* I could understand. But he didn't want me to take over the reins.

No, that particular honor would go to my brother.

Me, he just wanted under his thumb.

Which was why he'd bought Frank and Susan's company, effectively putting me out of my job.

It was also why he'd bought the building I was currently living in.

And why he'd had his business manager send me a letter stating he was raising the rent . . . to double my current rate. Oh! But my father happened to have a guest house available on his property and surprise, surprise, it was the monthly amount I was presently paying.

So, yeah no, I didn't exactly feel peachy about working for my dear old dad.

He had a vision of what my life should look like and when that didn't align with mine, he forced it anyway.

"I don't blame you," Seraphina said. "Just with everything going on—the baby, the job hunt—keep it in your back pocket in case you end up needing something fast."

I sighed. "You're right. Unfortunately."

"They don't call me The Brain for nothing."

"I don't think that's what they call you." I snorted and lay back against the pillows in my bed, tugging the blanket up to expose my feet to the cool air.

She *psshed,* and I could practically hear her rolling her eyes. "I need to get into work."

"Rub it in, why don't you?"

"Shush you and rest up. Apply for some jobs. You'll find something in no time."

"Hope so."

"Know so."

"Love you."

"Love you more," Seraphina said and hung up.

I sniffed, wallowing for one more minute about my circumstances before opening my laptop and pulling up a job search site.

"Anything close," I murmured as I began typing. I couldn't afford to be picky at this point in my life.

I sent my resume off to a minimum of twenty HR departments and five recruiters. I updated my professional profile on social media sites, threw together a quick website, hoping to drum up some freelance design work, and then spent a few hours searching for new apartments.

Two bedrooms.

Now, that was a trip down crazy lane.

With a sigh, I closed my laptop and sat up. I had snack wrappers littered all over my bedspread. It was my attempt at staving off the hypoglycemia as I worked, but the trash combined with bedhead, last night's jammies, and not having bothered with a shower, made me feel like I was one step away from eating bon bons and watching soaps.

I gathered the trash and went into the bathroom, cranking on the shower as I brushed my teeth and wrestled my hair into a ponytail.

I couldn't be bothered with an hour spent blow-drying my mop today.

Especially since I had absolutely zero need to look good for anyone.

When the shower was hot enough, I stepped in and rinsed off, shaving my legs and armpits. I used my expensive body wash, the one that reminded me of my father's rose gardens and the few happy memories from my childhood.

I'd loved to get lost among the flowers, a book in hand, wandering through the maze of planter beds. In the spring, color had exploded around me, a fairy-tale world straight out of a kids' movie. In the winter, the bare vines had looked almost menacing, a villain come to life.

I'd held tight to the escape from reality. In fact, I'd reveled in the chance to get lost in my imagination. Especially when everything else in my life was so cold and artificial.

Calculated.

A battleground.

With me in the middle.

I didn't want that for my baby.

Thankfully, I didn't have to worry about that. Jordan was long gone. My little raspberry and I didn't need the drama he'd no doubt bring to our lives.

It would be easier without him.

Nodding in agreement with myself—*don't judge*—I turned off the faucet and dried off.

Since I had no plans of leaving my apartment, I pulled on a pair of sweats and a "Taco Cat spelled backward is still

Taco Cat" T-shirt. I only bothered with a bra because my nipples were so sensitive that I'd probably poke out an eye if I didn't. Fuzzy red and green striped socks completed the ensemble.

I was a mess and that was totally fine because I was all by myself—

I shrieked and stumbled back against the wall, rattling the framed picture of Seraphina and me wine-tasting. I'd, of course, hated all the wine. Which was really not the point at all, I thought as I straightened the photograph and took a deep breath. The important part of the current situation was that my living room was full of suits.

And one of the suits was Jordan.

"Glad you could join us," he said coldly, eyes surveying me from head to toe in one slow glare.

I lifted my chin, the blatant dismissal I found on Jordan's face giving me the strength to ignore my uneasiness with the current situation taking place in my living room. "I wasn't planning on ever seeing you again, so consider yourself lucky to be in my apartment. How'd you get in?"

"You should be more careful about who you let see the code."

Perfect.

"Or maybe you should go fu—"

"Careful," Jordan said.

I sighed and leaned back against the wall. "What happened to you?" I asked softly. "For a moment, I thought we might have some fun together, get to know one another. Since, you know, we apparently made a baby together." I pointed to the room full of suits. Not one of them who'd deemed to take a seat on my couch.

They probably thought the used piece of furniture was beneath them.

I smirked, thinking that Jordan hadn't seemed to mind it during our night together.

"Apparently is the key word," he said.

Sighing, I pushed off the wall, feeling the rough abrasion of plaster against my fingertips before I strode into the kitchen and filled a glass with water. I took the prenatal vitamin the doctor had given me and chased it with a few crackers to prevent any nausea.

Less puking was a good thing.

The sound of a throat clearing didn't draw my gaze.

Or, I didn't *let* it. I was very aware of Jordan standing a few feet away in my kitchen, very aware that the suits were there for a display of strength and to intimidate me.

But I was the daughter of Bernie-freaking-Roberts. I didn't get intimidated. Not by a couple of junior lawyers who were in my apartment for show.

"One partner, one business manager, two lawyers who barely passed the bar, and one egotistical asshole of a baby daddy," I said, placing my glass carefully in the sink and turning to face Jordan.

"Did I forget anyone?"

He just stared at me.

I shrugged. "No? Okay then." I walked out of the kitchen and into my bedroom.

"Where—?"

I closed the door, cutting off the rest of his question and picked up my cell, dialing a number I didn't want to call, but one I knew I needed to.

"Bec? Can you come to my apartment?" I asked. "I've got an issue."

Her voice was crystal clear in my ear, a sharp New England accent with a side of no bullshit allowed. "What is it?"

"Suits. A baby daddy trying to intimidate me."

"Assholes. I'll be there in fifteen." Then, "You're pregnant?"

"Just found out yesterday," I assured her.

I could picture Bec's red lips pursing. "Okay, fine. Was going to give you shit for not telling me, honey. You know I'm prime godmother material."

I laughed, already feeling less on edge just knowing my friend, who also happened to be a hotshot lawyer, was on her way. "Godmother? Maybe minus the cursing."

"That's an important part of a child's education."

"If you say so."

"I *do* say so." A pause, then beeping followed by the rumble of an engine. "I'm on the road. You just ignore those asswads and let me do my thing."

"I can do that."

"Good."

She hung up and I sat on the edge of the bed, taking a moment to swap my fuzzy socks for a pair that matched my fancy outfit. Or at least a pair that didn't clash so horribly.

Then I went into the bathroom and calmed my mop of hair down, wrestling it into containment.

Also known as a bun.

When I came out of the bathroom, Jordan was standing across the hallway, arms crossed.

"We need to talk."

"Technically, I'd say we didn't *need* to, but I think in this you're right."

"Good." He pushed off the wall. "Come sit in the living room. I'll break it down for you."

There were way too many condescending factors in his statement for me to let any of them slide.

"You'll break it down for me?" I lifted both brows. "Do tell? Oh and maybe if you're going to invite me to sit down on *my* sofa, the least you could do was offer a girl some chocolate and a glass of water."

"Didn't know I was your slave."

I rolled my eyes. "Didn't know being inhospitable was a life goal of yours."

"This isn't my house," he snapped.

"Case in point," I snapped back. "So why. The fuck. Are you. Inside of it?"

"We need to talk."

"That, I think, is overrated," I said. "You're trying to threaten me into agreeing to some shitty contract that lets you off the hook for all responsibility. But"—I gestured at him to lean in—"I don't want anything from you, so you can take your shitty papers, your subpar lawyers, and fuck off."

"Subpar?" one of the suits said. "We're from Lincoln and Associates."

"Like I said. Subpar. My attorney is Rebecca Darden."

One of the suits went pale.

"Yeah," I told him with a smile. "I know."

Rebecca—Bec—was one of the most famous attorneys in the country. And, luckily for me, she also happened to be one of my closest friends.

I wrinkled my nose as I started to push past Jordan. He was wearing that disgusting deodorant again and the smell was enough to make me shudder.

Jerk was probably doing it on purpose.

I shot him a glare when he snagged my arm and halted my progress. "You smell like shit."

He laughed coldly. "You're insane."

"And you're a complete mindfuck! How did you go from nice and caring and sweet to . . . *this*?" I ripped my arm free. "When I say I don't want anything from you—financially or emotionally or otherwise—I mean it. I don't need you or your money or your suits. I am fine on my own."

I plunked down into my cozy armchair, avoiding the couch and the possibility of Jordan sitting next to me.

One of the suits wrinkled his nose as he sat on the worn leather sofa and extended a thick folder toward me. "You'll find our terms very favorable."

I set the contract on the table. "Does this contain a document eliminating Mr . . . .uh . . . " I trailed off, realizing that I literally had screwed a man, practically puked on him, certainly passed out on him, and still I didn't know his last name.

This was why one-night stands never worked out.

"Does this contract eliminate Jordan's paternal rights?" I nudged the folder with my fuzzy covered toe. "If not, it's of no use to me."

The suit looked at me for a moment before flicking his gaze over my head.

"Oh for fuck's sake," Jordan snapped. "We all know that she's using this as a ploy to get more money. Just have her sign the agreement and let's be done with this already."

My vagina was seriously never allowed to pick another man in my entire life.

"She will do no such thing," Bec announced, pushing her way through the front door.

"Is there anyone who doesn't know the code to your apartment?" Jordan drawled.

"I guess not," I snapped. "If you were able to get in."

"Okay, children," Bec said. "What seems to be the problem?"

"Jordan, here," I said, "apparently has a fat wallet and is afraid that I'm trying to take a chunk of it.

Bec froze, eyes wide, then she bent at the waist and started laughing. I crossed my arms, not nearly as amused. The rest of the room was silent, listening to her wind down from roaring laughter to chuckles to the occasional giggle.

When she'd regained control of herself, Jordan pushed off the wall and came to stand between us.

"Care to share what's so funny?" he gritted out.

"I'm sorry," Bec said, wiping a finger under one eye and picking up the folder on the coffee table. "It's just that anyone thinking our Abby is a gold digger is laughable."

Jordan frowned. "And why is that?"

"Because Abby is Abigail Roberts."

His jaw dropped open. His eyes scoured the room as though looking for a billboard that declared in bright flashing lights:

Abigail Roberts—daughter of a billionaire!

Then he focused back on me, something like regret trailing across his face.

"Touché, motherfucka," Bec announced, miming a mic drop.

"Language," I reminded her as she sat on the arm of my chair and started reading.

"You and your language," she murmured. "And the things we do for our godchildren." Bec started reading the document, ignoring the suits. "You're dismissed. I'll contact you with our response."

Her eyes flicked back down as she rapidly devoured what looked to be gibberish to my eyes.

After a moment of the suits not moving, she snapped her fingers. "You're dismissed."

And somehow, that got the men moving. They filed out of the apartment in rapid time.

All except Jordan.

He paused in front of my chair and glared down at me. "This isn't over."

"And you sound like a shitty villain in a B-movie," Bec said before I could reply. "I said we'd be in touch. Your"—her eyes drifted down, then up—"*services* are no longer needed."

Jordan's lips pressed tightly together, but he didn't say anything further. Instead, he followed his team of suits out of the apartment, slamming the door behind him.

I gave the men a few minutes to clear the area then stood.

"Where are you going?" Bec asked.

"To change the freaking code."

TEN

Abby

"OKAY, GIRL," Bec said when I came back inside the apartment. "You need to spill *all* the details."

She'd slid down and taken over my chair, so I plunked onto the couch with a sigh.

"There's not much to tell."

A snort was my only response.

"Look, I'm—"

I was interrupted by a knock on the door. "Oh, come on universe," I muttered, pushing to my feet and moving to answer it.

"It's me." Seraphina's voice was muffled. "The code's not working."

I opened the door. "That's because I changed it."

She breezed into the apartment, bending to kiss my check. "Because of the suits?"

I turned, glared at Bec, who shrugged as if to say, "I called her, so what?" She was still reading the documents and didn't bother to look up at us.

"Because of Jordan," I said. "He memorized the code and decided to let himself in."

Her brows pulled down, but she nodded. "So what's the new one?"

I told her and she smiled. "That was a good date."

"The best," Bec agreed.

It was cheesy, but I'd chosen the night of our senior prom. We'd all gone to the same private school and had blown off our jerks of dates to hang out together instead. We'd busted a few moves—and not very good ones at that—on the dance floor, only giving our aching, heel-wearing feet a break during the slow songs.

It had been goofy and fun and . . . one of the most enjoyable nights of my high school experience.

"Well," I said. "I ran out of good number combos and that one always sticks with me."

"Me too." Seraphina grinned. "Especially since I almost flashed the entire senior class."

"Strapless dresses aren't the best option for you," Bec agreed.

"Neither is dancing to Queen Bey's anthems in said strapless dresses," I added.

"That I learned the hard way," Seraphina said, and we all broke into giggles. She'd caught the dress before she'd fully popped out, but unfortunately, her *girls* wouldn't pop back *in* as easily.

We'd done some sort of crab walk, mad scramble to the bathroom, guarding her assets, and hadn't been able to get everything back into proper alignment until she'd been unzipped, secured, and then rezipped.

I didn't envy her breasts for anything.

"Plus, I can afford better bras nowadays," she said with a

laugh. "And I learned that strapless shouldn't be my first choice."

"The boys were disappointed by that." Bec smirked.

Seraphina snorted. "I'm sure they were." Her eyes met mine. "Nice try to distract us from the real issue, Ms. Abby, but it's time to dish. What's going on?"

I tilted my head to Bec. "Why doesn't the hotshot attorney tell me? I'm guessing it's not great."

"You're right," Bec said, putting the folder down. "He wants a paternity test—"

Well that wasn't a big deal—

"—and if he's proven to be the father, he wants full custody."

"What the fuck?" Seraphina said, but I hardly heard her.

Blood pounded in my ears, and my fingers went numb. "No," I said. "Hell, no."

Bec nodded. "That is definitely a hell no. But you know what this means."

I nodded. "Image is everything."

"Yup."

"I need a job." I sighed. "And a nicer apartment."

"You should call your dad," Seraphina said, then raised her hands in surrender when I glared at her. "I know, I know. And I get it, but if this is about jockeying for position and image, wouldn't it be better to have Bernie Roberts on your side?"

"Except he's never on my side for anything," I grumbled.

"There is that," Bec said, leaning back in the armchair and tucking her feet up underneath her. "I propose this. I'll put together a counter contract, and you'll use your trust fund to find a nicer apartment. Or hell, buy a house. Bernie can't rent control that."

"Oh!" Seraphina clapped her hands together. "I like it."

Bec rolled her eyes. "You're a goof." Then to me, she said,

"In the meantime, keep the job hunt up and if you don't find anything in the next two weeks to a month, then you talk to your father."

"Fine," I said, "be perfectly reasonable, why don't you?"

I didn't like the idea of opening up the can of worms that was my trust fund—it was my father's money, after all—but if I was going to use it for anything, I figured that it should be for my child.

"Being perfectly reasonable is my job," Bec said.

Seraphina and I both laughed. Bec waved us off.

"Okay, enough of that. Let's order takeout and watch a Hallmark movie."

"I'll make popcorn," Seraphina said and headed into the kitchen.

"Are you sure you have time for this?" I asked Bec. She was months away from making partner at her law firm and I didn't want to do anything to jeopardize her chances.

She rubbed her hands together. "Are you kidding? You know I live for this sort of thing. Mr. Jordan O'Keith is going to be drowning in paperwork."

"O'Keith?" I repeated, stomach dropping to my feet. "Please tell me that isn't his last name."

She opened the file again and studied it closely. "I can't do that." A pause as she glanced up. "Who is Jordan O'Keith?" Her eyes widened. "Oh. *Oh.* No. Abby, you didn't!"

"I didn't know!" I scrambled to my feet, running for the bedroom and my laptop. "Maybe it's a different one? That's a common name, right?" I pleaded, coming back into the living room, computer in hand.

Seraphina popped her head out of the kitchen. "What is it?"

I opened the browser, typed in "George O'Keith + Son" into the search bar.

"Oh, fuck," Bec said when the page loaded. "Your dad is going to kill you."

"He is so going to kill me," I agreed.

On the screen was a line of photographs of my father's mortal enemy.

In some of them, he was hugging Jordan, and seeing the two men side by side brought out their similar features.

Same eyes. Same hair color. Same build. Same smarmy personality.

Fuck my life.

ELEVEN

Abby

TWO WEEKS PASSED without another word from Jordan or his company of suits. Bec kept me posted on which paperwork she and the other lawyers were exchanging, but because she might as well have been speaking another language, I was unable to say more than, "That sounds great!"

In the meantime, I was house hunting and job searching, the latter of which I'd finally had some success in.

I was heading to a second interview for a tech company that morning. It specialized in research and development of robotics, and they needed someone to oversee their merchandising design.

I was excited. I'd met with the HR representative and the COO the week before to show them my portfolio and we'd clicked. The job seemed to have a lot of moving parts—management of a few junior designers, long-term project planning, and even an opportunity to stick with my roots and undertake some assignments myself.

It was everything I'd been searching for, and I really hoped they liked me as much as I did them.

Why did I suddenly have the image of a little girl standing on the sidelines waving her hands and shouting, "Pick me! Pick me!"

So not a helpful thought going into a very important interview.

"Abigail." The HR representative, Jessica, walked past the reception desk and greeted me with an outstretched hand. "Lovely to see you again. Heather and Rich are ready for you in the conference room."

I stood, shook her hand, and followed her. "How was your week?"

Jessica rolled her eyes to the ceiling. "Craziness! But that seems to be the M.O. these days. We were bought out about three months ago, and while most things have settled, there are still weeks where everything seems to fall apart."

"This was one of them?" I asked.

"Oh, yeah." She stopped at the entrance to the conference room and smiled. "Good luck. I hope to see you around the office in the future."

I smiled back. "Me too."

Jessica pulled open the door and made the introductions. I'd met Rich the previous week, as he was the COO. Heather, the CEO, was new to me, but I immediately understood that she was the most important person in the room.

My father had that air, the one that made people around him sit up straighter and jump through *all* the hoops to impress him.

I considered myself immune to that sort of presence, but even Heather made my heart skip a beat and my stomach—which had been relatively agreeable over the last two weeks—twist.

I hadn't puked since that afternoon, but my queasiness had been intense.

Still, I'd managed with small meals and a package of saltines in my purse.

Today that might not be enough.

No, dammit. I gave my brain a mental slap. *Cut the crap.*

Lifting my chin and swallowing down the nerves and nausea, I shook Heather's and Rich's hands then sat at the table.

I'd brought a few different things with me including some mock-ups I designed of their robotics line for kids. I'd taken some creative license, enjoying the project probably a little too much.

"What's this?" Heather asked, eyeing the small box critically.

"Oh," I said, a bit embarrassed. It wasn't manufacturer's perfect, since I'd printed it at home, but I'd been proud of the packaging I'd created. Now I wondered if it were too juvenile. "Rich showed me a few of the sample products your company has created for kids and I . . . ran with it a bit. I'm sure it doesn't align exactly with what you'd imagined since we haven't spoken, but this is what I came up with. I can totally change anything. This was just geared toward the six- to eight-year-old audience . . ."

I forced myself to shut up.

"Hmm." Heather picked up the box, turned it over, and raised a brow at Rich before setting it back down.

Well, I guessed I'd screwed up this opportunity.

Damn.

I'd really wanted to work here.

After an inner sigh, I forced the negativity down and straightened my shoulders. I would finish the interview with confidence and pride in my work. Who cared what some judgy CEO thought?

"This is the mock website I put together," I said, opening my laptop. "And some graphics for social media ads." I clicked around, showing them the various goodies I'd made. "Some short videos using stock footage and design programs. If we pursued this type of advertising, I'm sure the marketing department could film some original content and we'd make it look a lot prettier."

"I think it looks damn good already," Rich said, and pointed to my favorite graphic. "I like this one the best."

I smiled at him. "Me too."

"Hmm," said Heather.

Holy mother of Batman.

I kept the smile on my lips by pure grit. "So that's what I have. Did you have any further questions for me? Want to see anything else in particular?"

"No," Heather said.

"Okay then." I closed my computer and began stashing my materials in my bag. "Thank you for your time."

I zipped my bag, stood, and slung it over my shoulder.

"I know your father," Heather said.

"Mmm. That's nice." I shook Rich's hand.

"I thought you might be hype."

I extended my palm toward Heather. "Not hype. I like to make my own way, and I love to design. That's the beginning and end of it."

"Hmm," she said, and put her hand in mine.

"Yeah." Super original reply. But I shook her hand and turned to the door. "Thank you again."

Heather waited to speak until I was crossing the threshold. "Jessica will email you the official job description and salary-benefit package. If all meets with your approval, I'll see you in my office eight o'clock tomorrow morning."

My heart skipped a beat before speeding up, pounding

heavily in my chest. I turned back to the table where Heather was staring down at her phone. "I'll look it over and let Jessica know."

"Hmm," she said.

I peeked at Rich, who was smiling widely. He gave me a thumbs-up.

I nodded at him, said goodbye, then got the hell out of that conference room before Heather changed her mind.

"YES!" Seraphina fist pumped as she let me into her house. She would be accompanying me that afternoon on my thus far unsuccessful house hunt.

Though the realtor had supposedly found a few more options for me in the competitive market.

Near wine country and in a city with more millionaires than anywhere else on the planet meant that my trust fund only went so far . . .

Okay, that wasn't totally true.

If I splurged, I could probably buy half the town.

But I didn't like using the money in the first place—my father had made it, not me—and if it was just going to be the baby and myself, then I didn't need a gigantic mansion.

Unfortunately, there weren't too many non-gigantic mansions in my town. Not if I wanted to be in the best school district.

And with the baby on the way, I needed to be.

"This job sounds perfect for you!" Seraphina said once I'd showed her the description.

"The salary is kind of low," I said. In fact, it was barely more than what I'd made with Frank and Susan, and RoboTech was a big corporation.

"You could negotiate for higher," Seraphina pointed out.

"Yeah, I could," I said. "But I kind of feel like Heather is waiting for me to pull the 'Bernie Roberts' rich daughter' card."

"You think it's a test?"

I shrugged. "Maybe. Is that crazy?"

"Maybe?" Seraphina smiled. "But by the way you described Heather, I wouldn't put it past her."

"I know."

"Well, only time will tell. And now speaking of things unrelated to both time and craziness, you're a little pale," she said, and led the way into the kitchen. Once there, she handed me a sandwich and pushed me onto a bar stool at the peninsula. "Did you skip a meal again?"

My eyes flicked down at my phone, checking the digital clock on the home screen. "No. But I *am* hungry and tired. I'm sure the interview is what exhausted me. That was a lot of stress for one morning with the prep and then Heather spending the whole meeting *hmm-ing* at me."

"You kicked butt in that meeting, I know it." Seraphina filled a glass with water then sat down next to me. "Now tell me about the houses we're seeing."

"I upped my budget."

Seraphina smiled. "Please say enough so that we can be neighbors?"

"I'm not sure I've upped it *that* much." Her wrinkled nose and pursed lips made me laugh. "Pout much?"

"I want you to buy the house next door and then for you to just randomly pop over for coffee all the time. It'd be like *Desperate Housewives* only less desperate and more fun."

"*Desperate Housewives*? How old are we? That show came out like fifteen years ago."

"Fourteen, thank you very much." Seraphina set the glass down. "I've been bingeing it and it's fabulous."

"You're crazy." I shoved the last bit of sandwich in my mouth, already feeling more energized. I hadn't even known I was exhausted until I'd sat down.

The adrenaline from the interview, I guessed.

"We could binge it together, you know . . ."

"We could . . ." I said, not wanting to commit. Christmas movies I loved. Romcoms, cheesy Hallmark movies. Yes, yes, sign me up.

Dramatic TV shows, not so much.

"Or . . ." Seraphina's expression was way too innocent. "If you moved in *here*, we could watch the whole thing and all the other bad movies we want. We could share books. It'd be great, like being college roommates again."

"Sera—"

"And eat ice cream and stay up late and . . ." I waited for her to wind down, knowing that once she went on a tangent, there was no interrupting her.

"It would be awesome!" she finished on another fist pump.

And since my friend wasn't known for excessive fist pumps, I crossed my arms, raised a brow, and waited. "What's going on?"

"Nothing."

"Mmm hmm," I said. "Spill, girl. You know we tried living together in college and it was nearly the death of our friendship. We are not hospitably compatible."

"We're older now."

"And you're not telling me something."

She slumped, sighing as she rested her head in her palm. "It's really nothing, not compared to what you've got going on."

I reached across the cream-colored marble and put my hand over hers. "My drama doesn't trump everything that is happening in our lives. Your stuff is important too."

"What you're saying is that it's not all about you?" Her lips quirked into a half smile.

"Well, I wouldn't go *that* far . . ." I smirked. "Tell me."

"I was dating someone."

"For how long?" I asked, surprised she hadn't mentioned it. We shared everything.

"I thought he was—" She made a face and shrugged. "I—it's stupid now, but I thought he might be my HEA."

Apparently we didn't share it all.

I squeezed her fingers. "But how? When?"

"Since that day at the bar. When I got called into work. I was running for my car and literally ran into *Him*. Or who I thought was a Him."

Him was our code for that mythical man, the hero from our novels, the person who we'd run off with into our happily ever after.

A Him was a really big deal.

I gasped. "Why didn't you tell me?"

"You had a lot going on and—" She grimaced. "That's not fair. The truth was, I didn't want to share the fantasy with you. Not because I was worried you'd ruin it or anything," she rushed to say when I sucked in a breath.

Her words stung, but it wasn't about me in that moment. "It's okay."

"No. It's not like you're thinking." Seraphina stood up and began pacing around the kitchen, the glass-tiled backsplash glittering behind her as she walked. "I didn't want to share because I was worried it would all go to shit and then I would be sad, and it did g-go to sh-shit, and I *am* sad and—"

The doorbell rang.

"Damn. That must be the realtor." I stood up, pulled Seraphina into a quick hug. "I'll cancel with her and be right back."

"No." She blew out a breath, swiped a finger under one eye. "I can wallow later. Right now, since you won't live with me, I want to convince you to spend some more money and live next door."

"Are you sure?" I gripped her hands. "We can put on jammies and eat chocolate. I'll even watch an episode of *Desperate Housewives*."

"Tempting." She put an arm around my waist. "But you need a house more than I need chocolate."

I made the sign of the cross and hissed. "How dare you say such sacrilege?"

She snorted. "I love you, dork."

"Love you more."

The doorbell pealed again. "Come on," she said. "Let's go house hunting."

TWELVE

Jordan

JORDAN CLIMBED the stairs to Abigail's apartment and was surprised to find the door was wide open.

He frowned and peered inside, stomach jarring when he saw the living room was empty.

"Can I help you?"

An older man with a beer gut and blue coveralls came out of the hallway. He peered at Jordan suspiciously.

"I'm looking for Abby."

The man's mustache twitched. "She's at the doctor."

"What?" He took a step forward, feeling, for the first time in weeks, the frost seizing him shatter. "The baby. Is she okay?"

The man shrugged. "All I know is that she left in a big hurry." He turned to head back down the hall.

Jordan ran out of the apartment. He'd come . . . to apologize? To make her see reason? To get her to collar her bulldog of an attorney? His lawyer was complaining about an office full of briefs and filings and affidavits.

But Abby was at the doctor and that meant—

He sprinted for his car, stopping at the bar to beg the use of a phone so he could call his assistant.

"I need you to find out what hospital Abigail Roberts is in," he ordered when Brent answered. He pulled out his wallet and opened it to find the business card with the obstetrician who'd seen Abby in the hospital. "Check at Geary Regional first. Dr. Stephens. Call me back."

"For a man who says he doesn't need an assistant any longer," Brent said, "you sure call me a lot."

"Shut up and do it."

"Love you too. Give me five." He hung up the phone.

It only took Brent three.

"Suite 201, Geary. Dr. Stephens," he announced when Jordan answered the return call.

"Thanks."

"A thank you?" Brent asked with mock incredulity. "That might be the first verbal expression of gratitude in the history of all time you've—"

Jordan hung up, thanked the bartender for the use of his cell, and left the bar. He ran to his car, unlocked it, pressed the button to start the ignition, and tore off for the hospital.

The fifteen-minute drive was horrendous, one of the longest of his life. He didn't know why he even cared.

Relief should be coursing through him, not terror.

But . . . he did care.

It took him an agonizing few minutes to find a parking spot, during which time he seriously considered just leaving his car in the middle of the lot.

He didn't do that, one, because he wasn't *usually* an asshole and, two, because the car was brand new.

He'd upgraded to an SUV.

The one with the best safety reviews. He'd even had his assistant order a car seat and a crib.

Okay, so maybe he *had* been putting Brent through the wringer lately.

Jordan guessed it was a good thing his *unneeded* assistant was still on the payroll.

In any event, he parked the car and was hustling for the stairs less than a half hour after walking into Abby's apartment.

He pushed out of the stairwell, ripped open the door and . . . found a waiting room full of women.

All of whom glared up at him with narrowed eyes.

So much suspicion being thrown his way today.

"Can I help you?" the receptionist asked.

He gave her The Smile. The one that had always melted his nanny's heart, even when he was in deep shit for having eaten a gallon of ice cream.

It was the same one that usually got him whatever female attention he required.

Coincidentally, it was also the smile that didn't work on Abby.

But he couldn't think about that now. He had to keep his game face on, find out what was going on, and most importantly, he needed to remember that she was exactly like all of the other women in his life.

Exactly like the women who'd nearly ruined his father's business.

Who'd managed to successfully decimate his family.

"I'm sorry," he said when her look went from guarded to dazed. Yes, he'd mentioned before he wasn't *usually* an asshole, but he knew his effect on women and wouldn't shy away from using it. God knew the female population did it all the time.

Jaded much?

He stifled a sigh, leaned against the counter, and dropped his voice conspiratorially. "I was rushing in because I'm looking for Abigail Roberts. I've never been here before, and she's—"

The receptionist's lips curved up, her bright red lipstick jarring against the maroon of her scrubs. "Oh, of course. Don't worry, she was running late herself. Go on to the other door, and I'll send the nurse out to get you."

"Thank you," he said, moving to the side. The panic that had been gripping him eased.

The receptionist was calm. Surely if Abigail was in any danger, her demeanor would be more serious, or they would have sent him down to the Emergency department.

Maybe she just wasn't feeling well?

Which probably meant that he should just turn around and leave. It wasn't a crisis. He had no business being there.

Except . . . something inside of him would not let him leave until he'd laid eyes on Abby.

He needed to see for himself that she was okay.

"Here you go, Mr. Roberts," the receptionist said, using Abby's last name like it was his and they were married. He didn't bother to correct her, especially when she ran a hand down his chest and leaned so close that her breasts brushed his arm.

"Oh, I'm sorry," she said when he flicked his eyes down and raised one brow. Hurriedly, she stepped back. "Ms. Roberts will be in the second room on the right."

"Thank you."

"My pleasure."

The way she said those two words was not flattering. It was slightly creepy and very much over the top.

But he supposed that it was his fault for unleashing The Smile.

God, he *was* an asshole.

Instead of letting that stop him, Jordan walked down the hall and opened the second door on the right.

In retrospect, he should have knocked.

"Jesus Christ!" Abby shrieked. "What is it with you and trying to expose my vagina to the world? Get out!"

He stood frozen for a moment, round two of sights he could never unsee now burned on his retinas, before stepping through the door and closing it behind him. "Dr. Stephens," he said.

"Mr.— oh, you'll have to forgive me. I'm terrible with names."

"Jordan," he said, and released The Smile for the second time. Why not? He was already in deep with the receptionist. He may as well use it to get on the doctor's good side. "You can call me Jordan."

Dr. Stephens raised a brow at Abby. "Got a dangerous one there."

Abby snorted. "Yeah, and his sperm is the most dangerous part." She glared at him. "What are you doing here?"

"I went to your apartment."

She rolled her eyes. "I changed the code."

"The door was wide open," he countered.

The doctor coughed and Abby jumped. "I'm sorry—"

"Carry on," Jordan said. "I'll just sit over here and not bother anyone."

Another snort from Abby, but she didn't protest as he moved to the chair at her side.

"Cold," Dr. Stephens warned and then moved her hand under the paper blanket thing Abigail had draped over her legs.

Abby winced but didn't say anything, just turned her attention to the machine next to her.

Jordan's breath caught. "Is that—?"

Dr. Stephens smiled. "That's your baby. Here's the head and the feet and that little oval there is the heart."

He watched the rapid *flutter-flutter* of his baby's heart, heard the *whoosh-whoosh* as the organ pumped furiously on the black and white screen, and something unlocked inside him.

"Here." Dr. Stephens handed him a printout of the image. "For the scrapbook. Or wallet. Or whatever." She passed a larger stack to Abby. "Everything looks good. I'll see you in two weeks, okay?"

"Okay," Abby said.

"Keep it up with those small meals and call or email me if you experience any dizziness or fainting."

Abby agreed and the doctor left.

Jordan leaned toward Abby to get a better look at the ultrasound pictures, but she pushed him away.

"Are you serious right now?"

"I just want to see the pictures."

She shoved them into his hands. "Look all you want, but get away from me." She gulped, clapping a hand over her nose. "Haven't puked in two freaking weeks. Five minutes with you and I'm a hairsbreadth away. You're wearing it again, aren't you?"

"Wearing what?" He was barely listening as he flipped through the photos of his baby. *His* baby.

How was this his life?

"Satan's deodorant."

That got his attention and he shifted his gaze to Abby. "What are you talking about?"

"Your deodorant smells like shit." She stood up, careful to keep the drape around herself.

Disappointing, that. He hadn't seen nearly enough of her.

And he was fucking insane to go there. Even if it was just in his head.

"You just turn your back, mister," she ordered, shuffling

toward the pile of clothes on the bench. "Last thing you need to see is more of me."

He could argue the point, but Jordan opted not to.

Instead, he did what any normal man would do: acquiesced to Abby's wishes and shifted in the chair—then watched like hell out of the corner of his eye.

THIRTEEN

Abby

WHY THE HELL was Jordan there?

I pulled on my underwear and pants, moving quickly to get decent. The man had horrible timing.

"Okay," I said once I'd slipped on my sweater and boots. "You can turn around now."

Jordan spun in the chair, his long legs cluttering up the small space between the exam table and the wall. The room had been plenty big without him. Then he'd barged in and taken over.

I could smell him. I could feel him, his presence somehow radiating into the space between us and reminding me of the spark that was always there when he was near.

So far, that spark had brought me nothing but frustration and anguish.

I needed to remember that.

Because when he wasn't actively being a jerk, my body seemed to forget the fact that I hardly knew him and that he was batting at a less than ideal average, both in the bedroom activities—okay, *coffee table* shenanigans—and normal human inter-actions.

"Why were you at my apartment?"

He sighed. "Should we continue this conversation some-where that isn't a doctor's office?"

I huffed, slammed my hands on my hips. "Why, Jordan?"

"I want you to call off your lawyer."

I laughed and started for the door. "You're kidding right?"

"No, I'm not."

Turning the knob, I said. "Then you must just be stupid because I'm not calling off Bec—"

The rest of my sentence was cut off as a warm chest pressed me against the door, a slightly calloused palm covered mine on the knob. "I'm not stupid," Jordan said into my ear.

"A-acting like it," I said, forcing my idiot body to stop melt-ing, to stop liking the feel of him against me.

He was bad in bed.

He knocked me up.

He tried to take my baby away.

"Let me go," I hissed and struggled against him.

Jordan released me, backing up a step. His pupils were dilated, the black nearly eclipsing the blue of his irises. He raised his palms when I whipped around.

"What the hell is with you?" I asked, flattening my palms against the wooden panel of the door. "I can barely keep up with your moods. One second you want to fuck me, the next you're gone. Then you're back and I see this glimpse of a nice, caring guy who, oh, by the way, wants to fuck me again." I laughed but it wasn't filled with humor. "Then it's like whiplash because all of a sudden you hate me, accusing me that I'm a gold digger. We hardly know each other. I wouldn't invest this much time into managing some asshole's moods even if I *did* know him."

"Are you done?" he asked when I'd finished, chest heaving, cheeks hot.

Unbelievable.

"Yeah," I said and opened the door. "I'm done here. In the future, communicate through my attorney."

As I walked out of Dr. Stephens' office, I half expected him to stop me, but Jordan let me go, and I was relieved.

Really, I was.

He was insane, his moods yo-yoed faster than I could keep up with, and furthermore, he wanted to take my baby from me.

I forced a smile at the receptionist, making a note to call and speak to the manager about them letting Jordan in without asking me first, before hurrying out of the waiting room and into the hall. I found my way to the stairs leading down to the hospital's lobby and walked out to my car. But when I pulled the door handle, it didn't unlock. Frowning, I pulled again. I had one of those cars with the locks that automatically disengaged when the key fob was near, because, well, history told me repeatedly that keys and I didn't mix.

But the theory of automatic locks only worked when I had my purse. Or rather, my keys *in* my purse.

Which was likely sitting on the counter in Dr. Stephens' exam room.

Dropping my head back, I stared up at the clouds. November wasn't the coldest time in California, but the sky was gray and there was a definite chill in the air. None of which would help me get my purse back.

I was exhausted. I didn't want to walk back into the hospital. I didn't want to do a damn thing except cozy up on my couch with a blanket and a book. But I needed to go back to my apartment, make sure everything was moved out and locked up, and then drive across town to my new house.

Which was on Seraphina's street—actually directly *across* the street from her home. We were both excited.

Separate but close by worked for us.

Of course, none of this changed the fact that I still didn't have my keys.

I made a face, wanting to be in the jammies-on-the-couch portion of the day already without the rest of my adult responsibilities.

Unfortunately, life didn't work that way and with a sigh, I pushed away from my car.

"Looking for this?"

Jordan.

I made a sound, a whiny little cry that would indicate to any of my friends that I was nearing the end of my rope.

He didn't pick up on the signal. Instead, he stood there, my black purse gripped in his hand like it was a clutch rather than a good-sized handbag.

I'd forgotten how big he was.

Big.

I giggled at the absurdity of it all, especially when my thighs clenched and I felt moisture pool between my legs.

He was horrible in bed, you little hussy, I thought.

Well, not horrible so much as premature. With a little practice . . .

Oh, my God. I was going insane. It was the hormones. Had to be. All the books said that my sex drive might increase. *That* was the only reasonable explanation for why I could possibly still be attracted to him.

Jordan rattled the bag, like he was shaking a toy for a dog. Annoyance flared. Really? Should I trot over and rub myself on him in thanks?

My body liked *that* idea. Especially when the movement

lifted the hem of his T-shirt, exposing a couple of inches of hard, flat abs. It liked the rubbing-all-over-him option a lot.

I tilted my head to the sky again and tried to find my freaking brain.

I was losing it, switching personalities faster than the man in front of me.

But what could I possibly say?

"Come closer. Let me smell that Satan's deodorant of yours and remember all the reasons why I can't fuck you."

His brows drew down. "What was that?"

Oh come on, Abby, I yelled internally. *Filters. Stop allowing your thoughts to vomit all over the sidewalk.*

"Nothing," I said. Thank God I hadn't spoken loudly. "Just thanks for grabbing that."

"Did you say—?"

"Uh-uh. I didn't say anything. I most definitely did *not* say that my body is a confused asshole that still wants to have sex with you, even though you are maybe the worst lay of my life and—"

Oh. Good. God. I clamped my lips closed.

"You want to have sex with me?" Jordan closed the distance between us and I backed up until my spine was pressed against the cold metal of my car.

"I didn't say that."

One hand came up, caging me in. "I think you did."

"Nope." I lifted my chin. "What I *said* was that my body wants to fuck you. My brain, on the other hand, is very logical and understands that while you may be pretty to look at and have a rather large . . . *hammer*, you're not equipped with the knowledge to use your apparatus properly."

I smiled when his jaw dropped open.

"And let it also be noted that you're a jerk."

After snagging my purse from his limp fingers, I slipped

under his arm—gagged, because his deodorant was seriously the worst—and pulled the door handle.

Thankfully, the locks disengaged and I slipped inside, locking them behind me before Jordan got any ideas. I pushed the button to start the car, put the engine in gear and began reversing, forcing him to move back or get run over.

Unfortunately for me, he chose option A.

I glanced out my window just before driving away and saw that his expression was stormy. I could have sworn that his lips had formed the words, "I'm not done with you," but I pretended not to notice.

I was done with Jordan O'Keith. Once and for all.

FOURTEEN

Abby

MY BLACK PENCIL skirt was a little tight and I was struggling to suppress the urge to adjust it as I walked across the lobby toward the bank of elevators leading up to my new job.

Usually, I'd take the stairs, but RoboTech was on the fifth floor which was about four floors too many in the heels I was wearing.

"Ms. Roberts?"

I turned and smiled at the security guard. "Oh," I said. "Was I supposed to check in with you? I didn't realize—"

The younger man smiled, eyeing my too-tight skirt in a way that made me feel instantly uncomfortable.

"I've got your badge," he said, gaze most definitely not on my face. I knew I was a little extra boobalicious because of the pregnancy. My ass and breasts were the only parts of my body to increase in size thus far. "Mr. Sutter"—Rich, the COO—"said to give it to you. You'll need it to access the elevators."

I took it from him, feeling gross. This is why I'd begun to hate corporate jobs, why I'd worked at the graphic design firm with Frank and Susan. They'd had a family business, full of understanding and teamwork. With big corporations, the attitude and, often, the whole Mad Men-type climate that still existed in some circles, was deplorable.

One word to my father and this troll would *literally* be bankrupt, but I didn't equate being sleazy on the same level as ruining someone's life.

Unfortunately.

"Thanks," I said and reached for the pass. "If you'll just hand it over, I'll be on my way."

"You know," the guard said as he pulled the rectangle of plastic back and held it out of reach. "I have a lot of power here, and if you go out with me, I can show you how that power works."

Gross.

"I'm confused," I said, tilting my head to the side and blinking doe-eyed up at him. "How would you *show* me your power?"

A wink. "That's for me to know and you to find out." Barf. "But I do have keys to every office in the building. I have access to some . . . interesting projects."

And great, the guard had escalated from sleazy pickup lines to corporate espionage. Now I'd definitely have to report him.

I sighed, and his expression went from supremely confident to more than a little desperate.

Idiotic man-child.

Didn't he understand what he was saying?

Hadn't he signed an iron-clad NDA like I had? That paperwork alone should give any reasonable person pause. And he was just offering this up like candy to get a *date*? With me?

I stood by my idiot statement.

"I'll show you," he said when I didn't reply. "In fact, just the other day I went into one of the offices and saw—"

"You're fired."

My head whipped around. Heather stood there, furious.

"I—" His arms flapped at his sides, the desperation from the previous moment turning into pure panic.

Heather picked up her cell phone and dialed a number. "Stan. Get your ass up here. Now."

I bit my lip in nervousness when she hung up and stared at the guard. "Uh"—I hitched a thumb toward the elevators—"should I go on up?"

Heather shook her head fiercely and not one strand of her hair dared to disobey. It was pulled tightly into a bun that stayed perfectly in place. My ponytail—that I'd spent a good forty-five minutes attempting to wrangle into some semblance of control—looked positively messy in comparison.

"You'll stay." Her eyes flew up, pinning the guard in place with laser focus. "And you as well." A sniff. "For the moment."

Our trio stood there for an awkward ninety-six seconds—yes, I counted. Several people walked through the lobby, a few even pausing as though to offer help, but one shake of Heather's head sent them on the way.

I couldn't help but be mesmerized by the bun, or more realistically, how the bun didn't move a millimeter.

"What?" she asked, catching me staring.

My cheeks heated. "Sorry," I muttered. "I have hair envy." I pointed to my mess of brown hair, which I could already feel sliding loose. "Mine is hopeless."

She raised a brow.

"Totally inappropriate, I know." My nose wrinkled, knowing this was my boss, but not able to stop the verbal diarrhea, I continued talking. "But in stressful situations, I tend to focus on the minute details."

"Sharing flaws on your first day?" she asked, her mouth almost curving into a smile. "Most wouldn't risk that."

"I'm assuming you like me more for my work than my personality at this point," I said. "Might as well give you reasonable expectations to start."

Heather shook her head, but I definitely saw a smile. It lasted a whole four and a half seconds—yes, I counted again—before it disappeared.

A door behind the security desk flew open and a man with gorgeous olive skin came out. He was sporting a trimmed salt-and-pepper beard and had a network of lines around his eyes that made him appear more friendly than harsh.

"What's up?" he asked.

"Stan," Heather said, "meet Abigail."

He shook my hand. "Nice to meet you, Abigail. I'm Stan. I'm in charge of security here at RoboTech."

I nodded. "Nice to meet you too."

"Introductions made, let's get down to business," Heather said. She nodded at the nervous looking guard. "We've got another one and this one is extra stupid."

"Fuck," Stan said then winced. "Sorry. Not so much as for the language as for this asshole." He turned, gestured for another man to come from the back. "Go with Francis," he ordered. "Now."

"I didn't—"

"Diego," Stan said. "That wasn't an invitation for you to speak. Do yourself a favor, shut the fuck up, and go in the back."

The guard hung his head and I felt a moment's pang of guilt before I shoved it away.

This mess was his fault. Not mine.

"How many more are left?" Heather asked when he'd gone.

"Of the old staff? Two. But I actually like those two." He sighed. "Then again, I liked Diego, *or* I thought he had the potential to change."

"Mmm," Heather said. "If they step one toe out of line—"

"Gone," Stan agreed. "What specifically did Diego do?"

"Offered to exchange corporate secrets for a date with this one." She pointed at me. "Admitted to going into RoboTech offices to look at projects. Not to mention sexually harassing my new employee on her first day."

"Fucking moron."

"I mean for a minute there I actually felt bad for him," I said. "Then I realized he was a giant idiot."

Stan snorted, and I winced.

"Sorry, I probably shouldn't have said that."

"It's the truth," he said. "I'm sorry you had to deal with that. My company recently took over security and cleared house." He sighed. "Or I thought we had. That's not how I expect my employees to act. He'll be gone before you come down for lunch." His eyes tracked to Heather. "I'll talk to him, see what he knows."

"Make it clear to him what he'll lose if he chooses to blab again," she said. "Lucky it was here and now. All of these leaks need to be plugged."

Stan nodded and left them.

"Let's get to work," Heather said and led the way to the elevators.

FIFTEEN

Abby

"WELL, that was one way to make an impression," Seraphina said. It was just before lunchtime, and I'd spent the morning learning the lay of the land from Rich and meeting the staff who would be working for me.

Two senior designers. Five junior designers. Seven people for whom I was now responsible.

The notion was daunting—the most employees I'd managed with Frank and Susan's company was three and two of those had been college students on an internship. These employees were serious workers and enthusiastic about the projects they were designing.

"After lunch, Heather wants to meet with me to discuss timelines."

"Did she mention anything else about the guard?"

"No," I said, slipping my feet back into my heels and standing up. "But I also didn't ask. I got the feeling she didn't want me to, and since I'd been with the company for all of a half hour at that point, I didn't think it was appropriate."

"Getting someone fired in your first hour." Seraphina grinned. "Why do I think your father would approve?"

I snorted.

"Speaking of the elder Mr. Roberts, have you told him yet?"

"He knows I moved," I hedged.

Seraphina sighed. "It's going to be worse if he finds out from someone other than you."

"It's going to be terrible if he finds out from me."

"Abs."

"Sera."

Silence.

"I'm going to tell him."

"When?"

I turned to the window and sat on the edge of my desk. If I looked into the distance, ignored the streets and highways and houses and buildings in between, I could pretend the rolling hills covered in grape vines was my only view.

Somewhere up there, my father owned several wineries. His house was in those hills. As a kid, I'd spent more time running through the vines and the gardens than inside. It had been simpler. Quieter. Less imposing.

Less scary than dealing with my dad. No, less scary than *disappointing* my dad.

Of course, that was before I'd realized that everything I did would disappoint my father.

This was no different.

"I'll tell him."

Seraphina caught the change in my tone as any good friend would. "Abs, it's going to be—"

"I'm fine," I said, and forced my voice to be chipper. "I've got to go. Don't want to overshoot my lunch hour on day one."

"Are you sure you're—?"

"See you tonight?"

She blew out a breath. "See you tonight."

I hung up and blinked away the tears, knowing that it was the hormones making my eyes a little watery, not because I was torn up about my father and my childhood.

I was twenty-seven, for God's sake. A grown woman with her own life.

I could *not* have daddy issues.

I suspected I did anyway.

"Gross," I grumbled and picked up my purse. There was a soup and sandwich place just down the block. I'd fill up on some carbs and maybe splurge on a cookie.

I walked into the hallway, passing Heather's office, and nearly plugged my nose at the hint of sour in the air. It reminded me of—

Nope, not thinking about Mr. Thor Wannabe.

I breathed through my mouth until I'd gotten far enough from the scent that I didn't feel like puking. Hopefully, one of the staff didn't wear the same deodorant as Jordan.

After popping into Rich's office and asking if he wanted me to pick up something for him—no, since he'd brought his lunch —I took the elevators down to the lobby and walked out into the fresh air.

Today the sky was clear, but it was cold and I immediately regretted not bringing my jacket.

Still, it wasn't bad enough for me to go back upstairs. I toughed it out to the deli and ordered a salad and soup, sitting at a little table in the back while scarfing the two down and reading a book on my phone.

And I did splurge on a cookie. Double chocolate chip.

Belly pleasantly full and my body warmed from the soup, I headed back to the office.

This time no security guards accosted me on my way to the elevator. The extent of my excitement was when Francis—the guard who'd escorted Diego off to what I now imagined as a scary interrogation room, complete with two-way glass and intimidating lighting—smiled and waved at me.

I smiled back and got on the elevator. On the way up, I began regretting the double chocolate chip cookie. In the span of five minutes, I'd gone from pleasantly satiated to overly full. A good walk would have probably cured the feeling, I thought, and made a mental note to ask Rich where the stairs were.

The elevator opened with a ding and I stepped out onto RoboTech's floor.

My office was down the hall to the right, in between Heather's and Rich's. It had a glass door and a large window in the front. Both had blinds that could be closed, but I hadn't bothered.

Unless someone actually knocked—and even sometimes not then if I was really engrossed in a project—my focus was completely devoted to whatever I was working on.

There was still a trace of the smell in the air, so I hurried into my office and closed the door.

I plunked my purse on the table near the window pointing out to the vineyards and sank into my office chair. Immediately, I toed off my heels and stretched my aching feet. The black pumps might look amazing, but they were absolute torture to wear. And though they definitely appeared professional, I wouldn't be wearing them again.

Flats all the way, baby.

After the shoes, I was tempted to release the zipper on my skirt but figured that probably wouldn't send the right message on my first day.

With a snort, I logged into my computer and pulled up my calendar. There was a request for a meeting with Heather in a half hour to discuss the projects she wanted to move on and their timelines. It was to be held in the conference room directly across the hall from my office.

I glanced up, noted the blinds to that room were closed, and shrugged as I got back to work. My email account had been set up and waiting for me that morning and it was already filling with messages. I had the feeling that just managing my inbox was going to be a challenge.

I set an alarm on my phone for twenty-five minutes later and got to work weeding through the messages. There was the typical new hire paperwork, most of which I'd already completed. There were project descriptions and proofs, an employee handbook, and several requests from the designers for meetings the following week.

After putting all the requests in my calendar and seeing the lack of available space, I decided that it was a good thing I'd started on a Friday. I might need all of Saturday and Sunday to recover from the scheduling nightmare.

Hopefully things would calm down after I'd settled in and had a chance to meet with everyone. Still, I couldn't help but feel that this job was going to be trial by fire.

My phone buzzed and I jerked up from the computer, silencing the alarm. I slipped on my heels, gathered a notebook, pen, and my cell and crossed the hall. Unfortunately, I also got another sniff of the scent along the way. Jesus, was someone rubbing it on the walls? Why was it so strong?

Shoving down the nausea, I pushed through the door. The blinds were still closed, so I wasn't ready for what I saw.

For *who* I saw.

"What are you doing here?" Jordan and I said at the same time.

He jumped to his feet and closed the distance between us.

"No." I took a step back as his smell inundated me. My

stomach churned. I felt saliva pool in the back of my mouth. "Stay there."

"Why are you here?" He didn't exactly look happy to see me, but he also didn't appear angry.

"I work here," I said, swallowing hard and pressing myself against the door. The wooden blinds rattled and screeched as they moved against the glass. I turned, straightening them before I did real damage.

In. Out. Don't breathe through the nose. Do. Not. Puke.

"Why are you here?"

"I own this company."

"Owned," Heather said as I whipped around, noticing her for the first time. I hadn't been able to see anything more than Jordan from the moment I walked in. "You *used* to own it," she said.

Jordan's jaw clenched. "I still hold the majority of shares, Heather."

"Come sit down, Abigail."

I blinked at Rich's voice, feeling extremely overwhelmed, but nodded and crossed to the conference table.

"Mr. O'Keith, I'd like you to meet Abigail Roberts, our new Vice President of Design and Marketing." Rich's gaze shifted between Jordan and me. "But I suspect you two already know each other."

Away from Jordan, I found I could breathe a little easier. The nausea was still there, but it wasn't like I was going to poltergeist vomit in the next few seconds.

I might actually make it to the trash can if needed.

"No," I said. "I'm not all that familiar with Mr. O'Keith."

"Yes," Jordan said at the same time. "I know Abigail."

I glared at him. "You do not *know* me."

He raised a brow. "Are we going to do this here?"

"No." I sniffed, pulling out my notebook and taking the cap off my pen before looking around the room.

Well, I looked at Rich and Heather. Jordan I deliberately ignored.

Both of Heather's brows were up. Rich's eyes were darting between his phone and the rest of us.

"Let's get started, shall we?" he asked after a moment.

"Yes," I agreed, and if it sounded a little desperate then it was because I *was* a little desperate.

To forget that Jordan was sitting in the room with me.

To forget that Jordan's baby was currently cooking in my womb.

Jordan sat down next to me. Even though there was an empty chair between Heather and Rich, he just plopped down and invaded my space.

His slack-covered leg brushed my thigh, making me shiver, but his eyes were on Heather as she began talking. I couldn't concentrate on her words, not when he was sitting next to me, his heat seeping into the space around me, all Thor-like and handsome.

". . . don't you think, Abigail?"

I started, my eyes jumping from Jordan to Heather.

I had no idea what she'd been saying.

Fuck me.

"I'm not sure that six months is a reasonable timeline to bring something like the kids' robot to market," Rich said. "The engineers haven't finished the programming. We have to test it with our focus groups. Send out early versions to bloggers—"

"The coding is almost done," Jordan said, drawing my gaze back to him. "I'll finish it by Monday. Then the engineers need two months tops. That gives four months for focus groups and bloggers. That's plenty."

"Okay wait," I said. "So you'll want market-level packaging

ready to go in *two* months? We have nothing but a mock-up I made. Two months is not nearly enough time."

"Hmm," Heather said, making a few notes on her laptop.

"That mock-up you made is nearly perfect," Rich replied, leaning back in his chair. "I've been consulting with our manufacturers. We have the supplies to replicate it already available in our warehouses. It can be used with very few manipulations."

"All right," I said, nodding. "Just to be clear, do you want my focus to be this before all else? Because if there are indeed no major changes and we're using the design I laid out, I could probably get what we need in eight weeks. All the other projects will need to be back-burnered though."

"Heather?" Rich asked.

Another few taps on her keyboard, another "Hmm."

"Jordan?"

He inclined his head. "This needs to get to market as quickly as possible."

"Why?" I asked. "A kids' robot isn't exactly a new concept. What's the rush? Why not take our time and line up the toy for next year's Christmas season?"

Heather nodded.

Rich nodded.

Jordan frowned. "It needs to be out as soon as possible."

"If that's the case and we're being realistic here," I said, "I'm going to need to pull all the designers from their other projects and put them on this with me. Is that going to impact other deadlines?"

"No," Jordan said. "Our Christmas push has come and gone. We have nothing due until the spring."

It was my turn to say, "Hmm."

I couldn't figure out why this was so important to Jordan. Why was he pushing the project forward in such a rush?

Wouldn't it make more sense to hit the market during a major shopping season? Why did he want to release in May?

Something was off, but I couldn't pinpoint what it was.

"Use whatever resources you need," he said.

"You're overstepping your bounds," Heather interjected. "This isn't your company anymore."

"It was my company for a decade, Heather," he snapped. "And my R&D is what keeps it alive during lean times."

"We're not in lean times," she countered. "I'm signing the contract with the Army."

"Which is idiotic at best."

"You sold the company to me. You trusted me to make the best decision for its future when you took your payday and checked out," she said, her chin lifting. "All was well and good until you decided that you couldn't hack it doing nothing on a beach."

"Now who's overstepping?" He leaned forward in his chair. "You know damn well why the military is a horrible idea."

"No," she said. "I know why *you* think it's a horrible idea. What *I* see as a businesswoman is an opportunity for sustainable and stable income for the next twenty years."

"Fuck," Jordan muttered and shot to his feet. The action was so abrupt that I jumped, knocking my phone, notebook, and pen to the floor.

He and Heather froze, turned to examine Rich—who looked as uncomfortable as I felt—and me.

"We'll continue this later," Jordan said.

Heather closed her laptop and stood, much more calmly than Jordan had. If her spine was as rigid as granite, then that was the only outward sign of her being upset. "There's nothing further to discuss. You wanted out of the business side. You're out."

"I'm still the majority shareholder."

She strode toward him, laptop under one arm. "I will bring Dad into this, if I need to, bro." Heather walked past him.

"You wouldn't."

"Hmm."

Jordan rolled his eyes but didn't say anything further.

"And you know exactly what he'll say," she chirped. "Rich, a word in my office?"

Rich gathered his things and was out of the room in less than thirty seconds, leaving me alone with Jordan and his dark storm cloud of anger.

Yeah, that I didn't want directed at me.

Carefully and *quietly*, since Heather's words seemed to have triggered some sort of contemplative coma, I slid my chair back and knelt to pick up my notebook.

My pen had rolled under the table and I had to crawl underneath to retrieve it. I was on hands and knees, arm outstretched, fingers just grazing the cap when I realized I should have just left it.

I had a box of twenty-three identical others in my office.

"You're killing me in that skirt," Jordan said softly.

I gasped and tried to stand, which basically meant that I tried to give myself a concussion by cracking my head against the underside of the heavy oak table.

"Shit," he said and crawled under next to me. "Are you okay?"

"No," I groaned, collapsing on my side, one hand covering the aching spot on the back of my head. "Why would you do that?"

He touched my arm cautiously. "I didn't mean to startle you."

"Well, congrats." I glared over at him. "You did anyway, plus you messed up my hair."

He grinned. "I like your hair messy."

My stomach fluttered before I reminded myself of who exactly Jordan was. No flutters. Nope. No freaking way.

"Here we go again," I said. "Am I going to get Dr. Jekell or Mr. Hyde?"

"Neither." He crawled closer. "You're going to get Jordan. Just me, none of the other bullshit that's colored my past or our interactions. You're going to get the real me."

The words might have been considered sweet if I could have actually processed them.

But I couldn't.

Because Jordan coming closer meant that he'd exposed his armpit.

"Satan's deodorant," I gasped, clamping my hand over my mouth as the smell hit me.

Nausea roared and that too-full feeling from a half hour before exploded.

Literally exploded.

Everywhere.

SIXTEEN

Jordan

JORDAN DESERVED IT. Really, he did.

"Oh, God," Abby said, heaving again.

He shoved the trash can under her nose just in time, holding back her hair with his other hand.

Yes, he might have researched what to do if a pregnant woman was puking on the Internet. Yes, it should have been obvious before the search what to do.

But he was a guy. He didn't have a lot of experience with vomiting or pregnant women. And he definitely wasn't used to dealing with long hair.

He had congratulated himself on the wet towel thing when that came up in the search. *That* had been genius.

Well, technically it was his mom's genius since she'd done that for him when he was sick. His heart clenched at the memory. He didn't think of her often, not when it always hurt so much.

"Get. Away." Abby shoved him hard enough that he toppled

backward onto his ass. He barely had the presence of mind to let go of her hair.

"I'm trying to help," he said.

"You've helped enough," she gritted out. "Now stay out of nose-reach. Please. For the love of all that's holy."

He finally clued in. "Is it the deodorant again?"

Hazel eyes flashed up to his. "You think?"

Jordan pushed himself back until he was on the outside wall. From the waist up, he was covered in puke. It soaked into his shirt and he unbuttoned it, peeling it free. His undershirt had survived a little better, so he walked over to the sink, shoved the shirt into the garbage bin there, then washed his hands.

Luckily, his sense of smell sucked, otherwise he might have been joining Abby at the trash can.

"What can I do?" he asked.

She moaned and pushed the bin away, lying curled up on her side on the floor.

Jordan was a total dick for noticing her skirt had ridden up and that her panties were just a sexy as those four-inch pumps.

Which—he frowned—she shouldn't be wearing. Not in her condition.

What if she fell?

"Abby?"

"Shh," she said.

He fell silent, waited for her to say something. When she didn't, he cautiously moved across the room and glanced down.

Her face was flushed, her eyes were closed. At first, he thought she'd passed out again and his heart skipped a beat. Then her lips pursed, forming a little "o" as her breath puffed through.

She'd fallen asleep.

In a conference room. In the middle of the day. On her first day of work.

She was going to kill him.

He debated whether to wake her or not and after a moment decided not to. How could he? She was carrying his baby, and if she needed rest, then he'd damn sure make certain she got it.

But his conscience pinged as he slipped through the door, closing it behind him. He knew that the kids' robot project was going to put her under more strain and he knew he should extend the timeline or maybe table it all together.

Except . . . he couldn't do that.

"What are you doing?" Heather hissed.

When her eyes locked onto his shirt, blatantly eyeing his state of undress and the closed door behind him, he put his hands up. "Come on," he said. "Like I would ever have a relationship with someone in the workplace."

She raised a brow, pointed at his shirt. "Hmm."

"You and your fucking *hmms*. You think you sound smart by just uttering a syllable? Use words like a normal person."

"You want words?" she asked. "Why are the hell are you partially dressed after spending an extra half hour with an employee you obviously have a past with? Why does she hate your guts?"

He crossed his arms. "She doesn't hate my guts."

Heather laughed. "You're more delusional than I thought."

"It's not like that," he said. "We—" Jordan sighed, thought *fuck it*, and laid all the cards on the table. "She's pregnant. It's mine."

"Uh . . ."

For once, Heather using only one syllable didn't annoy the shit out of him.

"You—" She shook her head, dropped her voice. "You fucking idiot. You're kidding me, right? Don't you know who she is? Who her father is?"

"I know," he said. "Well, I didn't know that night. But I, uh, learned a couple of weeks ago."

"And this project. *This* project we have her on. Don't you realize how that's going to look—" She put up her hand, eyes widening. "Wait. Did you say you *just* learned who she was?"

"No, I found out weeks ago."

"Before or after?"

He rolled his eyes. "Before or after what?"

"Before or after you found out she was pregnant?"

Jordan hesitated, and Heather groaned, pacing away a few steps before turning back toward him. "Oh, my God, you're a bigger idiot than I've ever given you credit for. You did it, didn't you? Acted just like Dad."

"I— It wasn't like that—"

His sister pretended to hit her head on the wall. "It was. You did exactly what Dad would have done. Tried to pay her off." She started laughing. "You tried to buy off Abigail fucking Roberts."

"Shh," he said. "You'll wake her up."

Heather's laughter abruptly halted. "My new VP is asleep in there?"

"My mere smell makes her puke."

His sister started giggling, albeit quieter this time. "Oh, this is too good."

"She's exhausted," he said, and if his tone was accusatory, it was because he felt no little amount of guilt about the stress he must have caused her over the last few months. Leaving her that night. Serving her with papers. Being a total asshole at every opportunity.

"I'm not going to fire her," Heather said. "She's the best designer I've ever met, *and* she seems to be good at managing people."

"I don't want you to fire her," he retorted, crossing his arms and leaning back against the wall of windows next to the door. "Just cut her a little slack."

"Don't fuck this up for us. If you want your pet project to go, we need to keep her happy."

Jordan sighed. "Noted."

"So why isn't she on Roberts' payroll?" Heather asked.

"Unlike Dad, good old Bernie doesn't like women on staff."

The lights above them turned on automatically, telling them both that it was getting late. The office generally closed early on Fridays since many employees worked longer days during the rest of the week, so the space was quiet.

"Dad liked women on staff a little too much."

Jordan smiled ruefully. "That he did."

"Bernie's missing out."

Jordan nodded. "I know. Today was the first time I'd seen her work. It's genius."

Heather didn't say anything for a long moment, just studied him closely before shaking her head. "Careful, brother, or you'll end up like Dad, a brood of half-bloods gathered under his wing."

"Just because you have a different mother doesn't mean that you're not my sister." He paused, made sure his words were calm when the anger in him was a real thing. His past—his *father's* past—did not define him any longer. "And I'm not Dad. When I'm with a woman, I'm only with that woman.

"I know." She patted his arm, eyes warming for a brief second before her normal devil-may-care, taking-asses-not-prisoners demeanor returned. Another shake of her head. "You knocked up Abigail Roberts. What a fucking idiot."

And with that sisterly idiom, she walked away.

Jordan listened to her pack up her stuff in her office,

watched as she walked by. "I sent Rich and the others home," she tossed over her shoulder. "Lock up when you leave."

He nodded his thanks and sat down to wait.

SEVENTEEN

Abby

MY NECK ACHED, and there was a very persistent, very annoying buzz coming about six inches from my left ear.

I groaned and rolled over, wondering when my bed had gotten so uncomfortable.

Groping for the phone, said source of annoying, persistent buzzing, I blindly swiped my finger across the screen. "Hello?"

"Are you okay?" Seraphina's voice was concerned.

"Yeah, I'm fine," I said. "I was just tired so . . ." My words trailed off as my eyes adjusted to the dark room.

This could not be happening.

"I'm sorry!" Sera said. "It's just that I got home and saw your lights were off. I didn't realize you were sleeping. Go back to bed and call me later."

She hung up before I could say anything in reply.

Which was a good thing, because the fact that I'd fallen asleep after puking my guts out in the company conference room on my first day of work was a fact that was not going to be spoken about until I died.

I banged the back of my head against the floor then whimpered when the sore spot connected with the hard surface.

"This literally cannot be happening," I moaned, pushing to my feet. My shoes were lined up like a pair of perfect soldiers next to the trash can, both of which had been moved closer to the door.

I started for them and almost ate shit as a jacket I hadn't felt draped around me, slipped to my feet.

It was a man's jacket. Jordan's. I knew that because it smelled like him. Not like that terrible deodorant, but like Jordan the man. Slightly spicy and with a hint of salt. There was nothing sour about it when I brought it to my nose and sniffed.

And now I was randomly sniffing objects that belonged to my baby daddy.

Psycho, much?

I gathered up my notebook, cell, and pen, all of which were piled nicely by where I'd been laying.

I felt a wave of embarrassment flow through me. Not only because Jordan had seen me puke again, but also because everything my father said was proving to be true.

The weaker sex. Unable to hack it in a corporate world. Pathetic.

If he could only see me now, I thought sarcastically.

There was no way I still had a job after this.

Bending over, I grabbed Jordan's jacket and then walked to the door to snag my shoes.

I'd write my letter of resignation and email it to Heather.

I sighed. Not even one full day on the job before I'd screwed up. Classic.

Jacket draped over my arm, notebook, pen, cell, and shoes gathered in my hands, I struggled to open the door.

After a moment, it pushed inward a couple of inches.

My stomach dropped, all hope of slinking out unnoticed

vanishing.

"Hey," Jordan said.

I hooked an elbow in the door and opened it all the way. "Hey." I couldn't even meet his eyes, I was so embarrassed.

I slipped out into the hall and hurried to my office, flicking on the light as I did so.

Quickly, I dropped my things onto my desk, shoved my feet into my shoes, and picked up my jacket. I was just thrusting my arms into it when I heard Jordan's voice.

"Are you okay?"

I dropped my head back. Why couldn't the man let me wallow in peace? I was beyond embarrassed. I wanted the floor to open up and swallow me whole. I wanted—

To be left alone.

Instead of saying any of those things, I forced a smile, finished buttoning my coat, and grabbed my purse. "I'm just peachy."

"Abby . . ."

So what if my throat felt tight? So what if my eyes burned? I was just fine, dammit.

I sniffed, closed my eyes hard, and lost the battle with tears.

They poured down my cheeks in hot tracks and I quickly turned around, not wanting Jordan to see. Everything else was awful enough. This was just that extra cherry on the sundae he didn't need to see.

Chin to my chest, my foot tapping on the floor in pretend irritation—because it was actually tapping in my-feet-really-fucking-hurt-and-it's-still-not-as-painful-as-the-ache-in-my-heart —I said, "I'm totally fine. You just go ahead."

Okay, that sounded watery. But, hell if it was all I had in me. "Dammit!"

I jumped, whirling around.

Jordan was five feet away from me, his hands at his sides and clenched into fists. "I want to hold you but I can't because I make you puke!"

I laughed.

Because of the absurdity of the situation. Because it was better than crying. Because I couldn't do anything else.

I laughed until my stomach hurt and I slid to the ground. I laughed until Jordan started laughing too. And finally, I laughed until he sank to the floor across from me, safe-smelling distance away.

"If you just changed deodorants—"

His smile took my breath away.

Suddenly, I couldn't look at him. My eyes drifted from the window to my desk, to my feet . . . back to Jordan.

"Hi," he said softly.

"H-hi." Oh, my God, I was such a dork. My voice was shaking and my fingers were trembling. I felt like we were on the precipice of something huge and I couldn't decide if it was good or bad.

"Can we maybe try to start over?"

My thumbnail had a chip in the red polish adorning it. Actually, my pinky did too. I needed to redo all of them. Maybe in blue? No. That wasn't really office-y. I could do silver sparkles. That would be pretty and just in time for Christmas. I—

"Abby?"

I straightened my shoulders, forced my gaze to his. "I'm not sure how to do this," I admitted. "We haven't exactly had the best start."

"I know," Jordan said, "and it's my fault."

"Not going to disagree with you there," I muttered.

He laughed but then went sober. "Can I tell you something? I think it might help make sense of everything. Not that it's an excuse, but just . . ."

I studied him as he trailed off. "Give some clarification?"

"Yeah."

"Okay."

"I—" He stopped. "It's just that—" A shake of his head. "Damn, this was easier in my mind."

My heart started beating faster. I wasn't sure if it was because he was uncomfortable or because what he was about to share was something big. I just knew that he looked nervous and I felt for him. "I know the feeling." He glanced up. "Of things making more sense in my mind than in real life."

He tilted his head to the side, eyes piercing as they locked on mine. "I don't know how I ever thought that you could be like them."

I picked at the hem of my skirt. "Like who?"

He grimaced. "Like the women I grew up with. No," he said when I frowned. "Like the girls my father slept with after my mother died."

"I'm sorry," I said. "I didn't realize you'd lost—"

"It was a long time ago and it's not important."

"Well, it's clearly important." I crossed my arms. "Otherwise you wouldn't have brought it up."

Jordan smiled again, this time not the take-my-breath-away version, but a sadder, smaller one. I didn't like it.

"You're right," he said. "It *is* important. My mom was the glue that held my family together."

"How many of you are there?"

"There were four of us. Now there are two."

My brows drew down. I knew Jordan's dad was still alive and Heather had called him brother. Maybe that was a nickname?

"I see you're mentally calculating," he said. "There were four of us before she died. My mom and dad, Zach—who was two years older—and me. After my mom . . ." His eyes dimmed, blue becoming icy cold with sadness. "Well, my dad's drug of choice to forget was women. It got worse when Zach died five years ago."

"How old were you when your mom . . . ?"

"Eleven." He rolled his eyes. "Zach was sixteen. Both of us saw the never-ending parade of women—of *girls*, really, they were barely legal—coming through the house."

My stomach twisted itself in knots, my heart absolutely ached for the little boys who'd lost their mother and then, for all intents and purposes, their father as well.

"I'm so sorry."

Jordan shrugged. "It was what it was. I stopped blaming my father for it a long time ago. And I got some pretty cool half-siblings out of it."

"How many?"

"Six. Well, seven, including Heather." A pause. "You're doing that mental calculating thing again."

I froze. "What?"

"When you think really hard, these pull together." He scooted a little closer, near enough to reach up and brush the skin between my eyebrows before dropping his arm and sliding back. "Okay?"

I sighed, still able to feel the brush of his fingers on my forehead. The skin was warm, marked by his touch. "Yes," I said, breathless, and felt my cheeks heat.

"I like touching you."

I ignored that, wanting to lighten the mood instead. I liked it when *he* was on the spot, not when his focus on me. "Lovely," I said, rolling my eyes. "Just thinking is going to give me wrinkles."

"I can smell the smoke," he said.

I snorted.

"Not to mention, it's cute. *You're* cute. Well, you're beyond beautiful, but then you make a joke about yourself or start talking about marketing and design and my breath catches. You're so much more than the outside."

That was the dream, right?

For someone to see me as more than just the sum of my parts. For someone to see inside my heart and decide that I was worthy of being loved.

God, I was so fucked up.

Not a shocker, given my past. But instead of focusing on the uncomfortable feelings blooming inside my brain and body, I concentrated on Jordan.

Why was he doing this?

Did he really want to start over?

Realistically, I wasn't sure I could. I'd seen so many versions of Jordan at this point that I wasn't certain which was the real one. How could I reconcile the kind, thoughtful man in front of me with the jerk surrounded by suits in my apartment?

How could I trust that he wouldn't change right back?

"You're doing it again."

I reached up, felt my wrinkled brows, and relaxed my forehead. "I don't know if I can start over."

He grimaced. "I understand. I'll leave you alone."

But despite our words, neither of us moved.

I stayed still, watching him watch me and decided that while I couldn't be certain he wouldn't revert back to asshole Jordan 2.0, I was also quite certain that I was willing to take the chance.

"Heather doesn't look younger than you," I said, and it was a question even if it wasn't phrased as such.

"She isn't."

"Then—"

"She's six years older."

I frowned and felt it that time. Dammit, I *did* do that a lot.

"My father was with her mother before mine. We didn't find out about each other until she was eighteen."

I whistled. "I bet that was dramatic."

Jordan's lips twitched. "Considering she crashed a dinner my father was throwing for his shareholders, yes. It was quite the moment. Though"—he shrugged—"she was the third half-sibling that I had found out about, so not much surprised me at that point."

"Still must have been hard."

"Everyone has their own challenges. My father's is, apparently, wrapping his tool."

"Gross," I said, laughing.

"Yeah, tell me about it. My father's youngest is four years old. The man is sixty." He shuddered.

"I bet he gets a lot of grandpa comments."

A smile. "Like you wouldn't believe. But I think it's well deserved. His last mistress—he doesn't even bother getting married anymore—was younger than me."

"Yikes."

"I know."

"Okay." He sighed and pushed to his feet. "Well, that's enough about me. It was a dick move to assume that you'd be like them. I've seen the custody, alimony, child support thing pan out a half dozen times now." He raised one palm. "Not an excuse. There was no excuse for my behavior. Just an explanation."

I nodded.

"I'll wait for you in the hall. Walk you to your car, if that's okay? I'd feel better knowing you were—"

"My parents are still married," I blurted.

He stopped, hands at his sides, and stared at me.

"I haven't seen my father since last Christmas." I swallowed. "As for my mother, I haven't seen her in fifteen years."

EIGHTEEN

Abby

I TOOK A DEEP BREATH. Aside from Bec and Seraphina, no one knew this part of the story.

Not my brother. Not my father. Neither of them could understand why my mother had run.

But I did. Intimately.

"You ready for the big guns?" I asked.

"Big guns?"

I swallowed, already feeling a little shaky at the prospect of admitting this. But Jordan had laid his past out for me. He deserved to know why I tended to keep people at a distance.

"You ready to hear why I'm so fucked up?" I asked. "Because it's a doozy."

"You don't have to—"

"I do," I said. "I tend to hide in my own world because of it, and if we're going to have a baby together, you need to understand why I sometimes engage the hard retreat." My lips trembled and I pressed them together tightly.

Jordan froze, face serious. He nodded tightly and sat down a couple of feet away from me, back against my desk.

I shifted so my shoulders were resting on the wall below the window.

"Okay?" he asked.

"What?"

"The smell." He pointed at his armpit.

The tension in my gut uncoiled slightly. "Don't worry, you're out of smell-shot."

He snorted. "I'm throwing away this deodorant as soon as I get home."

"That would be much appreciated," I said.

And then there was no avoiding it. I just had to say it. To get it out there.

"I was eleven when it happened." Jordan's eyes shot to mine, and I forced my lips into a rueful smile. "Eventful year for both of us, I guess, huh?"

My legs were flat on the ground, still in the heels.

Jordan rested his palm on my ankle, glancing down at me.

I nodded. He waited for me to find the words.

"I was really into gymnastics and I was really good. I'd just moved up a level and had a new coach. I was practicing my splits—it was the one thing he said I was behind on." I stared down at my hands. "And me being me, I just had to work on it until I had it. I—" My voice broke.

Jordan squeezed my ankle lightly and the touch brought me back to the present. Away from that night. Away from that room.

"The coach took me from the main floor to this room that was walled off from the rest of the gym. No parents went back there. Not that mine would have come anyway. They were too busy with their own lives. They didn't have time to waste on something as insignificant as their daughter's gymnastics class."

"Abby."

I was shaking, but made my eyes meet his.

"You don't have to do this."

I nodded. "I do. I haven't—I should have done something. I found out about five years ago that he'd gone to prison for molesting girls. But the dates were ten years after he'd done it to me." A tear streaked down my cheek. "He touched little girls for ten years because I didn't do anything. Because I believed when my mother told me it was my fault. Because I was too ashamed."

"It's not your fault."

"I should have told someone else. I should have pursued it."

"You were eleven."

My head dropped to the wall. "I know."

"Did he hurt you?" Jordan's words were soft, but there was a deadly edge.

"No. Well, not physically. He had me get into the splits and I remember him kneeling behind me, resting his hands on my shoulders—the coaches did that sometimes, put a little pressure on you to help the stretch—but then he took it further. He slid his hands up and down my arms, down my chest. I hardly had boobs at that point, but I remember him probing, rubbing at what little I had there." My voice cracked. "I remember freezing. I remember feeling that it was wrong. But most of all I remember feeling ashamed."

I carefully met Jordan's gaze, wondering if I'd find the same expression of disgust I'd seen on my mother's face.

There was nothing there. He was staring forward, unseeing, and not one emotion was discernable in his expression. Not anger or revulsion. Not pity or fury.

Just nothing.

Then he blinked and saw me looking. "What did you do?"

"I told my mother. She said I was making the whole thing

up." I clenched my fingers together. "I found out later that she was sleeping with him."

Jordan's chest rose and fell in a long, slow breath.

"She never did anything. In fact, she forbade me from telling anyone. Said I was a slut who'd asked for it." I swallowed. "I know better now, but it took me a long time to confide in anyone."

"What'd your father do when he found out?"

"He doesn't know," I said. "You, Bec, and Seraphina are the only ones who— It's stupid, but every time I tried, I just pictured my mother's face. The disgust. I couldn't disappoint him that way." I laughed, bitter. "No, I found plenty of other ways to make him unhappy with me."

"That can't be true."

"It's true. But that's a story for another day. I switched studios and ended up quitting gymnastics altogether when he came into the new gym one day as a guest coach. I panicked, lied to my father about losing interest, and shoved the events deep, deep down." I sniffed. "If only they'd stayed there."

"Pain has a way of resurfacing."

I nodded. "That it does."

We were silent for a long moment before Jordan spoke again. "I'm admitting defeat on the whole starting over thing."

I laughed. "I didn't realize you were still stuck on that."

"Like a dog on a bone." He squeezed my ankle again. "How about instead of starting over, we move forward?"

"Throw out that deodorant, and we've got a deal."

———

Jordan was quiet as he walked me to my car. The air was cold and our breath blew white clouds as we crossed the parking lot.

I would have been just fine on my own getting to my car, but honestly, I was glad he was there. It was dark and I felt raw on the inside after sharing so much.

Given the tentative way he held himself, I suspected he felt the same way.

"Thanks," I murmured when we got to my car. I pulled the handle and the car unlocked with a beep.

"No problem. So . . ."

"Give me your phone," I said, reaching into my purse and snagging mine. "I'll get your number and text you with the information about my next appointment with Dr. Stephens."

It was a peace offering. And perhaps a way to move forward like he'd suggested.

Jordan rocked back on his heels. "See, here's the thing—"

I flushed, shook my head, shoving my cell back into my purse. "Oh. It's okay. You don't have to go. I just thought—"

"I don't have a cell phone," he said. "I threw mine away after I sold the company."

"You *threw* away your phone?"

"Not you too," he said, rolling his eyes. "Everyone is so glued to those damn things these days—and believe me, I used to be one of those people—but when I sold the company, I promised myself that I would take a break from all that. That I'd look up from my screen every once in awhile."

"I get that," I said. "But what about an emergency or if you really need to get a hold of someone?"

He smirked. "Don't know if you know this, but nearly everyone on the planet has a cell phone."

I laughed. "Okay, so you can't give me your number. How are we going to communicate to do this *moving forward* thing?"

"Landlines?"

"I haven't had a landline in years."

"Reasonable point," he said. "Email?"

"Which you could access better from a phone," I teased.

He leaned against my car, close enough to make my stomach flutter, but far enough to not trigger my bloodhound of a nose. "What's with the phone obsession?"

"Cell phones are great," I said, espousing on the merits of phones rather than investigating the underlying attraction that never seemed to go away when Jordan was near. "They play movies and hold thousands of books. You can text. And maybe even call someone on it."

He laughed. "All of that is true. So tell me," he asked, "what's your favorite book?"

"Which is like the world's hardest question!" I said, turning to match him, my shoulder resting against the driver's side window. "But if I had to pick one"—I reached into my purse and pulled out a worn paperback—"it would have to be *Pride and Prejudice.*"

"What do you like about it?"

I ignored the fact that we were having this conversation in the parking lot. That both of us should get into our cars and go home. I focused on nothing aside from the fact that he seemed genuinely interested in my answer.

"I guess I love that deep down Darcy and Elizabeth are perfect for each other, no matter that their circumstances and personalities attempt to keep them apart."

"Hmm."

"Now you sound like Heather."

He laughed. "Can't have that." His fingers laced with mine. "So tell me, how is it that you can't find your keys, but you can find your phone and book in that black hole of yours on the first try."

"Priorities, I suppose."

His thumb brushed against my palm. "I wish I could kiss you right now."

My heart leapt. Did I want him to? Did I dare risk pursuing

something with him? Our situation was already complicated enough with the baby and now work. Not to mention the fact that our fathers hated one another. "O-oh. I—"

"I'm not going to because"—his lips twitched—"Satan's deodorant, and I don't want to get puked on again."

"That was *not* my fault."

He brought our laced hands up, pressed a kiss to the back of my hand. "I'm not saying it is. In fact, I think if we're going with pop culture references, wouldn't all of this be my fault?"

"Yes," I grumbled. "It *is* your fault. Well yours, and also the manufacturer of my IUD since they promised baby-free sex and then didn't deliver."

A gust of cold air blew around my legs, up my skirt. I shivered.

"I should let you go," he said. "You're cold."

"Yeah," I said.

But I didn't want to go. I wanted to stay. I wanted to talk to Jordan all night.

"See you Monday?" he asked.

I nodded then winced. "Though I should probably turn in my resignation. With our relationship and your sister working here, not to mention the puking and the whole falling-asleep-in-the-conference-room thing, I didn't exactly make a good impression on my first day." I wrapped my coat a little tighter around myself. "That's not even considering the interaction with Diego."

His face went thunderous. "What happened with Diego?" Then he waved a hand. "Never mind. I'll find out from Stan." He squeezed my hand. "Who, by the way, can arrange an escort to your car if you're ever here late and I'm not and you're uncomfortable. Not that you would be uncomfortable working here, or want me to walk you to your car regularly. Or, well, that you couldn't take care of yourself. I just meant if—"

"Jordan." He stopped talking. "I understand." A beat. "Thank you."

"And Heather already told me she wouldn't accept your resignation."

"What?"

He nodded, pushed up to standing. "So there's that. You're working here and that's final."

I gave him the look. "Are you pushing it? Or just trying to be funny?"

"Maybe both?"

I huffed good-naturedly. "Men."

"We're exasperating, I know." He released my hand and I ignored the fact that I missed the warmth of his touch. "So Monday?"

A nod. "Monday."

He opened my door. "Good night, beautiful."

He waited until I was buckled in with the engine started before he closed the door then turned and walked back into the building.

I couldn't help but feel as though a piece of my heart went with him.

NINETEEN

Jordan

JORDAN STRODE BACK into the office and used his badge to enter the security office. Walls of television screens showed cameras from all angles. Every elevator. Every hallway. Every entrance and exit.

Stan glanced up from his desk, unsurprised since he'd been able to watch Jordan's approach the entire way. The light from the computer monitor made RoboTech's security chief's skin appear pale and ghostly. "Hey, boss. What's up?"

"Don't let Heather hear you say that," Jordan said with a smirk. He skipped the pleasantries. "What happened with Diego?"

Stan sat back in his chair. "He took the bait."

"Damn. I liked that kid." Jordan sighed and leaned against Stan's desk. "Any word on where he's trying to share it?"

Stan shot him a look. "Shouldn't I be discussing this with Heather?"

"Probably." He crossed his arms. "But discuss it with me too."

"Same buyer as three months ago. Wants specifications for the drone."

"And did Diego get them?"

"The ones we planted?" Jordan nodded. "Yup. I've got my guys trying to track the buyer. They're slippery as always, but the transaction has got to be clumsy if the hormone-riddled moron was using it as fodder for picking up girls."

"Girls?"

Stan shook his head. "Girl. Not plural. Abigail Roberts."

"He hit on Abigail?" Jordan's voice was a growl. Pathetic, but there it was.

"Who wouldn't?" Stan asked. "Not only is she gorgeous but that body—"

"Shut the fuck up."

Stan froze, eyes narrowed as he studied Jordan. "Something we need to discuss?"

"Nope."

"Abigail is a nice girl," Stan said.

"And how would you know?" Jordan said. So what if it sounded like an accusation? Who the hell was Stan to say such a thing?

A flash of humor crossed the other man's face before it went blank. "I worked security for her father about five years ago. Doubt she remembers me since she wasn't around much. But it's kind of hard to forget her . . ."

"I'd be careful with your next words."

"You've got a big ego, O'Keith, if you think you could take me," Stan said, amused. "But that's not what I mean. There's something vulnerable about her. I didn't like seeing the hurt in her eyes."

Neither did Jordan. Especially when he was the cause of it. "Yeah."

"Her dad is kind of a dick."

Jordan snorted. "I know the feeling."

"That you do." A pause. "So the specs?"

He released a frustrated breath. This whole thing was a fucking mess.

"They won't do the buyer any good. They're flawed and incomplete."

"You know that," Stan said. "*I* know that. But the rest of the staff doesn't. And they're getting pretty ballsy if they're entering Heather's office to steal information."

Jordan rose to his feet and thrust a hand through his hair. "Keep the last two around for a bit, see if they get pinged and are stupid. It might give us the information we need."

"Might not," Stan countered. "It's a risk."

"We've got to plug the leak."

"Thought you were supposed to be on a beach right now. That this all was Heather's problem."

"Things change."

One brow went up. "Not *that* much."

"It's complicated."

A smirk. "It's a girl."

"Abby is not a girl—" Jordan grimaced at the omission.

"So, Abby, is it?" Stan's smirk grew into a grin. "You know what your father would say about that."

"Something disgusting, no doubt." He sighed. "I knew the interest from the Army was a bad thing."

"It's a profitable thing, from what I understand."

"But at what cost?" He shook Stan's hand, headed for the door. "They never bring anything except frustration and heartbreak."

"How's Hunter?" Stan asked just as Jordan reached the threshold.

"How do you think?"

The last thing Jordan saw before heading up to his office was Stan's face creased with sadness.

He knew his own face was a mirror image.

———

"DONE," Jordan announced, pushing into Heather's office. He was bleary-eyed, hadn't left his desk except to grab food and pee since Friday evening.

He hadn't had a weekend like that in a long time, and though he was exhausted, it came with exhilaration. He'd figured out the issue with the code, and he'd finally finished the program. It was running flawlessly.

His previous position as CEO hadn't allowed him the joy of finding a problem and then a solution and following both to their fruition in a long, long time.

And the action brought with it a sense of completion he hadn't realized he'd been missing.

Okay, that wasn't quite right.

He knew he'd missed the grunt work. He knew he'd wanted to get back into the ranks.

He just expected to want that after a nice long break.

A few months ago, he'd been near burnout. No creative juices flowing, no new ideas. He'd been ready to throw the whole company into the fucking ocean.

Then Hunter.

Then Abigail.

Then Heather offering to buy into the company and taking over the business side.

Meetings and schmoozing and finding investors had been the worst part of his job, but he'd always figured he was good at it. The buyout offer falling through the night he'd been with Abby had proven otherwise.

The investor he'd planned to sell to had managed to turn key members of his staff against him, and they were stealing projects that were RoboTech's—then InDTech's—bread and butter.

They'd successfully taken a piece of programming that had been the company's future.

Not that he could prove it.

But Stan would, Jordan had no doubt of that.

In the meantime, Heather had bought him out. She'd taken over the company, renamed it, and cleaned house. All typical behavior of a buyout, except she'd kept those loyal to them and weeded out the rest.

Or so they'd thought.

Now three months down the line, Jordan wondered how many snakes in the grass were still out there.

"Done with what?" Heather squinted up from her computer screen and blinked. "Holy shit, you look terrible. What'd you do? Not sleep for the last forty-eight hours?"

"Yup," he said, his voice almost giddy from lack of sleep. "I'm done with the program."

Her jaw dropped open. "You're done? That's it? Two days when the rest of the crew has been working for weeks to figure out the glitch?"

He sank into a chair and propped his feet on her desk. "Yup. That's because I'm the best."

She shoved his feet off. "You're also delusional from lack of sleep."

"Maybe. But the program is airtight." He stood. "Have the crew test what's on the secure server."

Heather took his meaning right away. The program was there, or part of it, but the key was in his possession and his alone.

"Will do."

"You good with that?" he asked.

She gave him a look. "I trust you, Jordan."

The words made his heart give a little squeeze. "Yeah?"

"Plus"—her smile was evil—"I know *you* know that I'll cut you in your sleep if you screw the company over."

"So violent."

"You know it." Heather stood, kissed his cheek. "Get some sleep." Her nose wrinkled. "And take a shower. You smell."

"Noted. See you tomorrow."

She said goodbye and turned her focus back to her computer, dismissing him before he was even out of the room.

Jordan didn't mind. In fact, he respected the fact that his sister was such a good CEO. It reminded him that not all women were like those his father managed to get tangled up with.

He closed the door behind him and strode out into the hallway. It was early still, the workplace just waking up as staff trickled in. This had always been one of his favorite times of the day. The hum of a few computers, the quiet of only a couple of voices. Later the space would be awash with activity, punctuated with laughter and ringing phones, but this was the time that reminded him of the early days. Of scraping by, refusing to use his father's money to start the business, hoping on a dream that he'd make enough to pay the rent, let alone make millions of dollars.

Back then he'd slept in the office, kept his clothes in the one and only closet, bathed in the sink, hauled his laundry down the street to a Laundromat.

That had been before he'd owned an entire building, before he'd employed hundreds of people.

Before he'd flamed out.

Jordan shook his head and walked toward the elevator. The

lights were off in Abby's office, but he tried to convince himself that he wasn't disappointed at not seeing her.

It was probably better anyway. He hadn't been home to shower and smelled horrible. God knew what that would do to Abby's stomach.

He pressed the elevator button, head shooting up when it dinged straight away.

The doors open and Abigail started to walk off, only to stop and stare at him. "Jordan? Are you okay? You look terrible—"

"I'm fine. Just worked all weekend." He smiled and took a step back, aware of his smell all over again. There was no way he was making Abby puke again.

She came closer and frowned. "You're wearing the same clothes. No, is your shirt different? But your pants—you haven't gone home?"

"Got caught up with a project." She reached for him and he put his hands up to shield her. "Stay back. I haven't showered in two days either. I keep a spare shirt in my office, but that's it. I smell and don't want to make you—"

Her head tilted to the side, glancing down his body and back up. The slow perusal set his blood on fire and he suddenly wasn't tired any longer.

"You"—she sniffed—"smell *incredible*."

"What?"

Abby came close, her nose brushing against his throat as she inhaled. "Mmm," she moaned. "If you smelled like this all the time I'd rub myself—"

Jordan coughed, put his hands on her arms, and gently set her away from him. He was rock hard and aching. "I—uh. As much as I like it when you do that, this probably isn't the place."

She put a hand to her forehead. "I'm sorry. Whew. Is it hot in here?"

"No," he said, concerned now. "Are you okay?"

Her hand dropped. "Besides feeling like an alien took over my body? Hot. Cold. Aroused. Puking. This ride isn't for the faint of heart, let me tell you." She gave an awkward laugh and turned for her office.

He snagged her hand, slipping the briefcase she carried free of her fingers and taking her purse from her shoulder. "I'll walk you."

"Don't get too close," she said. "You might regret it."

"That, I doubt."

They strode in silence down the hall to her office. She opened the door and flicked on the lights. "Thank you."

"You're welcome." He handed over her bags, hesitated when she turned her back on him and went to the window.

"I used to play out there, you know?"

He frowned, crossing the room to look out the window. Busy streets bookmarked by multistory buildings for as far as the eye could see. "Were your parents insane?"

She smiled. "Sorry, no. I meant there." She pointed way out in the distance, to the vineyard-covered hills. "My father has an estate there."

"Mine too," he said. "Did you play in the vineyard?"

"All the time. And the rose gardens." Her face turned toward him. "Hide and seek was the best. Though"—her expression dimmed slightly—"now that I think about it, no one ever found me. I always thought it was because I was the best hider, now I'm thinking that they probably didn't want me underfoot."

"Abby—"

"No," she said, "it's okay. I'm not going to get all maudlin about it. I'm well aware that my childhood was firmly in the realm of fucked up. But damn, how much of a dick move is it to send your daughter out for a game and then not follow her?"

"A big one." He paused. "But, I have to admit, I'm guilty of sending my siblings off to play a game without intending to join in."

"I think *siblings* is the keyword here." She grinned. "How many of them lived at home?"

"All six of them still do. It was quite a rude awakening to come home from college and be assaulted by a gaggle of three to five-year-olds." He grimaced, thinking of those brutally early mornings and being barely twenty-one. Going out, drinking too much, hungover, and. So. Much. Screeching.

"Does your dad share custody?"

"This probably isn't the best conversation for us to be having"—he gestured to her stomach—"in our current situation."

"No," she said. "But I want to know anyway."

"Of course you do." He sighed. "Get ready for *The Jerry Springer Show* but in real life."

She straightened her shoulders, turned fully to face him. "Okay, I'm ready."

"I'm not sure if I am," he muttered. "But here goes. Six baby mamas, six kids. Of those, two became wives, then ex-wives. Those two still live at the house, albeit in separate wings." He rolled his eyes. "According to my father, they've bonded over what a jerk he is."

Abby snorted.

"I interpret that snort as agreement." Her lips curved into a full-blown smile and, *damn*. When she smiled at him like that, it took his breath away. "God, you're beautiful," he said.

Another snort. "No distractions, mister. You've started the family drama, you can't stop in the middle of the story."

"I could talk all day about family drama, just so you know."

"Oh, *I know*," she said. "Believe me. I know. What's with rich people and so many skeletons in their closets anyway?"

"Too much money, not enough common sense?"

She laughed. "I think it comes along with the trust funds." Her face went serious and she gripped his arm. "Promise me we won't screw up our baby. Promise me that we'll raise a well-adjusted, normal kid."

"God, I hope so."

He couldn't help himself, not with her so close. Not with roses swirling through the air and images through his exhausted mind.

Abby's stomach swollen with his baby. Abby holding a little girl with brown curls and hazel eyes. Abby in his bed. Abby smiling up at him like she was doing now. But she was in a wedding dress. She was *his*.

Jordan was spinning out of control. It was too much, these feelings that were developing. He should be running the other direction.

But he found he couldn't.

And when Abby's tongue slipped out, wetting her bottom lip, he couldn't resist.

He *had* to lower his head.

That first touch of his mouth to hers was explosive. Desire flamed low in his gut, his mind demanded that he move quickly, that he strip her clothes off and kiss every inch of her. He wanted to set her on the edge of her desk and lick her until she came. He wanted his fingers, his *cock* inside. He wanted—

She whimpered and all of that heat tempered.

Because he also wanted to love and stroke. To trail his fingers across her belly, to press his mouth to the place their child grew. He wanted to cup her breasts, kiss her throat and the spot behind her ear he'd discovered that first night.

He wanted to make her come so many times that she was limp and satiated and their first horrible evening together was forgotten.

Horrible for her, that was.

His orgasm had been life-changing.

Hers had come from batteries.

She deserved more.

He gentled the kiss, soft brushes of his tongue, gentle nibbles of his lips. He teased and coaxed until she was soft and limp, resting against his chest.

And when he pulled back and she looked up at him, those hazel eyes warm, he felt a piece of his heart go off into the abyss.

This was a woman a man fell in love with.

Her lids slid closed, her arms slipped around his waist, and she inhaled deeply.

It was the perfect moment . . . until she stiffened and stepped back, hand coming up to cover her nose.

"Satan's deodorant," they said at the same time, and smiled.

Hers was rueful. "I'll just sit over here," she said, and plunked down in her office chair, rolling it a few feet away.

"I should let you get settled."

"Nope."

His gaze flicked to hers, took in her amused expression. "What?"

"Don't think you're getting off the hook that easy, mister. I need the rest of the baby mama drama if I'm going to have a hope of focusing for the rest of the day."

He laughed. "You're ridiculous."

"Nope," she said again. "I just love *Real Housewives* and this is definitely on par with that. So the two ex-wives live at the house?"

Jordan shook his head but acquiesced. "Plus, one ex-mistress. Along with Parker, Steven, Mitch, Gabrielle, Victoria, Theo, and Hunter—my nephew."

"I didn't realize Heather had any kids."

"Hunter isn't Heather's. He's Zach's. Or was Zach's." Jordan forced his voice to stay neutral. It had been years. He should be used to it. "My brother was killed in Afghanistan five years ago."

Abby winced and stood up, crossing to him. She took his hand. "Oh Jordan, I'm so sorry. I didn't realize that he'd . . ."

She trailed off and Jordan squeezed her fingers. "It was a tough time for all of us. We didn't find out about Hunter until a year ago."

"How old is he?"

"Seven and a half."

"Damn." She sighed. "I'm sorry. That seems so inadequate but . . ."

He squeezed her fingers. "Thank you."

"What branch of the service was Zach in?"

Jordan stared out the window. "He wasn't. Zach was a contractor with the Army. My father sent him over to keep an eye on their company's prospects."

Her inhale was rapid and pained. "Oh, Jordan."

"I know."

"So the argument with Heather about the contract—"

He rubbed his free hand on the back of his head. "I shouldn't have gotten into that with you and Rich in the room. It wasn't—"

She hugged him. Tight. For a long time.

Long enough for the strain in his shoulders to relax minutely, for his arms to come around hers. Long enough for the ice around his heart to begin to melt, for the dark, heavy hurt about his brother to recede slightly.

"I'm breathing through my mouth, I'll have you know," she said, startling him into a laugh. "I promise I won't puke on you again."

"I think I deserved it," he said.

"Oh, I *know* you did. But a girl's got to have some pride, you know?" She loosened her grip slightly and leaned back. "Thank you," she said, softly. "For sharing that with me."

He brushed a strand of hair off her face. "I hope you're adding that to my positive points column," he joked.

"You've been adding to that for a little while now."

"I really should let you get to work."

"One more thing." Abby bit her lip. "Never mind. I've already been way too nosy."

"What is it?"

Her cheeks flushed, she opened her mouth, closed it. "I was wondering about the other kids' moms, is all. Wanted to complete my real-life reality show binge."

"The other three weren't interested in being parents. They took a payoff and signed over all parental rights." He smoothed his thumb over the streak of red on her cheek. "But that wasn't the question you wanted to ask and we both know it."

"I—"

He cupped her jaw. "It's okay, sweetheart. If we're going to make a go of this, then we need to be open."

"That's just it," she said and dropped her arms, stepping back from his hold. "I don't even know what *this*"—she pointed between the two of them—"is. Are we dating? Are we trying to get along for the baby's sake? Are we nothing more than strangers who got to know each other a little by pure accident?"

"We're more than strangers," he said, "and you know it."

Her chin dipped forward. "I'm not really sure what I know anymore. A week ago, I hated your guts. Today I want—"

She broke off, shook her head.

"Abby." He waited until she looked at him. "Today you want what?" Another shake of her head, but he moved close, refused to let her avoid answering the question. "What do you want, sweetheart?"

"Dammit." She blew out a breath. "I want you. *Okay?* And

not just your body—which I want to lick like a freaking Popsicle —but the rest of you. Or the part that I've gotten to know over the last couple of days. The sweet and thoughtful man who carried my briefcase into my office without asking and shared his past with me even though it was painful." Her breath came in rapid exhales. "I want the man who kisses me like I'm precious and who looks at me like he wants to tear my clothes from my body. And"—her shoulders slumped—"I find that I can't even dislike the man who was a jerk in my apartment. Not when I understand the context."

She fell silent as he was struggling to digest all that she'd said.

"You like my body?" he asked.

"That?" she nearly shrieked. "I admit all of that, and you're focused on that fact that I love your abs?"

He nodded, a smile tugging at his lips.

"You're unbelievable." She turned away, grumbling, "You don't even know how to use your hammer—"

He growled and pulled her close. "I know how to use it. I just need a chance to prove it."

"Been there, done that." She crossed her arms with difficulty since he'd snaked his hand around her waist and was holding her against his chest. "If I puke on you, it's your fault," she warned.

"Noted." He brushed his mouth against hers. "Abby?" Her stare met his. "I feel all of that too. And more. I want you. I picture you in my bed, in my shower, in my kitchen. I want you against the wall and spread out on your desk. But I also want the woman inside." He touched a finger to the spot above her left breast. "The one who I'm still getting to know. The one who has a huge heart. The one whose eyes get sad when she thinks about her past and the one who isn't afraid to sass me."

"I—"

He touched a finger to her lips. "Let me finish?"

She nodded.

"I like you so much that it's scary and I know that the stakes are high because of the baby, but I want to spend time with you. I want to know what irritates you, what makes you smile. I want you to show me the books that have made you cry, and I want to pummel every ex-boyfriend you've ever had." He held her gaze. "I want that coach to burn in hell, and I want to see you cradling our baby. It's crazy. I know it's too soon, but I can't stop myself from wanting to take the chance."

Jordan dropped his finger.

"I can't—"

His heart sank.

He should have known. These types of feelings didn't exist in real life. Not in *his* life.

"—stay away from you."

Her words hit his gut with the force of a blow.

"What?"

"Can we try?" She lifted a shoulder, her face earnest, her eyes laced with fear. "I think we owe it to ourselves to at least try?"

"Yes." He hugged her tight. "We need to at least try."

TWENTY

Abby

JORDAN PAUSED as he headed to the door of my office. "What question did you really want to ask me earlier?"

My heart was both raw and hopeful, and though I knew it was probably a nosy question, I asked it anyway. "Where is Hunter's mom?"

His blue eyes frosted over. "Left. Couldn't handle it."

"Handle what?"

"Hunter is sick."

My hand came up to my throat. "How sick?"

Jordan shook his head and I knew. *I knew*.

"I'm sorry."

I dropped my gaze to my hands. Such inadequate words. So useless. So *stupid*. Why had I pushed?

"Abby?" I glanced up.

"Thank you for caring."

I nodded. "Go get some rest."

He started to leave, paused again. "Dinner later?"

"I don't know what time I'll get off," I said, feeling behind already. I'd come in an hour early and that time was now gone.

Not that I'd take any of it back, I just knew that this project was important to Jordan and didn't want to screw it up.

"Email me when you're done."

"And you'll, what, be waiting around for my message?" I rolled my eyes and sank down into my office chair, rolling it with my feet close enough to my desk to reach my keyboard.

"Something like that," he said with a smirk.

I sighed. "You know there are advantages to having a cell phone."

He crossed his arms, leaned against the doorframe. "Name one."

"Sexting."

His jaw dropped open before he turned to leave.

"Where are you going?" I called.

"To get a new phone," he called back.

Laughing, I shook my head and got to work.

I SHUT down my computer and stretched my arms behind my head.

"All right?" Rich asked, knocking on the doorframe.

"I'm great," I told him honestly. "I'm loving this job."

"Two days in and you've still got the rose-colored glasses on?"

I laughed. "So far, so good."

"You out of here?"

I nodded.

"Cool. Me too. I'll walk you to your car, if you don't mind. I wanted to pick your brain about the placement of the new logo on the website."

"Sure," I said. "I noticed the parking lot was pretty dark on

Friday."

He nodded. "I just approved a work order for new lights. They're due to start the end of the week. In the meantime, have someone walk with you."

I slipped my feet into my flats and picked up my purse and briefcase. "Is there a reason that everyone keeps mentioning that?"

"We had a few robberies around the time of the buyout. I think that's why Heather brought in the new security." He lifted a shoulder. "I haven't heard of any issues lately, but I don't think it hurts to be cautious."

"Of course." I flicked off my light, smiling. "And thank you."

He smiled back. "It benefits me, you know. I get a little more time with that graphic design genius brain of yours."

I scoffed. "I'm far from a genius."

"How about a natural? If you won't give me genius, then at least give me that."

"You're a charmer, aren't you?"

He grinned. "Twenty years ago and minus one wife. Yes. Nowadays, I stick to honest."

My cheeks felt hot, but I ignored them . . . along with the compliment. We walked down the hall, and Rich pressed the button to call the elevator. While we waited, I asked, "Doesn't this building have any stairs? I feel like I'm always waiting for these metal death boxes."

He snorted but nodded to a door I hadn't noticed before. It was tucked into the corner near the bank of elevators. "Right there. But this old man has bad knees, five flights and I wouldn't be walking for the rest of the week."

"Oh no," I said. "What happened?"

"Football. And too much of it."

The doors dinged open and we got on. "I hear that can be a brutal sport."

"It sure can," he said, then grimaced. "Without risking monopolizing your after-work hours, can I get your opinion on the logo placement?"

I pictured the mock-up of the website the junior designers had emailed just before the end of the day. There was a lot of good in it: fun colors, clear tabs and font, but the logo wasn't right.

"I don't think it's the placement so much as the proportions. It's too big."

Rich pulled out his phone, accessed the link, and held it up so I could see the screen. "Damn, if you're not right."

"Words a woman lives to hear."

"Don't I know it?" We shared an amused gaze as he put his phone away.

"So tell me about this wife of yours."

"Well, she . . ."

I listened as we rode down, laughing at Rich's description of his wife and kids and their latest vacation, then at the misadventures of a new puppy at home that the three kids "just had to have."

"So then the dog took off through the house, one stiletto in his mouth, a pair of my daughter's underwear around his neck, just as she and her new boyfriend walked through the front door."

We were both chuckling as we walked off the elevator and into the lobby.

"Oh." Rich paused then patted my arm. "I don't think my escort services are needed. See you tomorrow." He turned for the exit.

I hardly saw him go.

Because my eyes were on Jordan.

Whose smile took my breath away. I found that I couldn't make my feet move, not toward him, not away. I just stood still and waited for him to approach, my heart thudding. *Thump-thump. Thump-thump.*

"Hi," I whispered when he was close.

"Hi." He put out his arms as though to hug me. "No deodorant. I promise."

I laughed, the spell that had surrounded me shattering. "Thank God for that."

"I got something for you," he said, taking my briefcase and my purse, slinging the former over his shoulder and holding the latter in his fist. I marveled again at how he made it seem so small.

Then again, what was the saying? Large hands, large . . . hammer?

I huffed out a laugh and Jordan gaze skimmed over me.

"You'll have to share what's so funny with me later," he said.

"Not happening." I grinned when he frowned. "What are you doing here? I thought you were waiting for my email."

"With bated breath." He tangled my fingers with his. "Don't you want to know what I got you?"

"Sure. But I like surprises too."

"Noted." He released my hand and reached into his pocket.

What he pulled out made me laugh.

"Isn't that more for you than me?" I asked of the shiny new cell phone.

"It is if you hold up your end of the sexting bargain."

My cheeks went red-hot. "Now wait a minute. I never said —" I broke off when I caught his mischievous expression and smacked his chest. "You're terrible."

"You like it," he teased and held the door for me as we left the lobby.

"Nope." But I did. I liked this version of Jordan a whole lot.

I could only hope he stuck around for a long, long time.

Or maybe even indefinitely.

TWENTY-ONE

Abby

"THIS ISN'T EXACTLY what I had in mind," I said an hour later.

Jordan had conned not only my cell number but my new address out of me before we'd left the parking lot.

"You said you were craving Chinese."

"That's not what I'm taking issue with," I said, pulling takeout containers from the brown bag Jordan had brought in.

"Then what is it?" he asked before starting to go through the cupboards. "Plates?" he asked.

"They're not unpacked yet," I admitted. "I couldn't lift the box. I've been using paper ones."

"Hmm." He pulled out his phone and pressed a button. "Hey, it's me. Yeah, yeah. Can you arrange the movers to come out and unpack the boxes Abigail has left?" He glanced up at me, brows raised. "What time?"

"I'm fine," I said, plunking my hands on my hips. "I'll get to it—"

"Why should you have to?"

"Because I—"

He turned his back on me, probably because he knew his next statement would piss me off. "Six tomorrow night. She'll tell them where she wants everything. They do all the heavy lifting." A pause. "Good."

Jordan tucked his phone away in his pocket and gave me a look that should have belonged to a little boy. It was guilty, full to the brim with remorse. The only thing missing was a toe making a hole as it dug into the ground.

I sighed, all the annoyance I'd felt in the previous moment slipping away. "You're lucky you're cute, you know that?"

His expression turned obstinate. "Well you shouldn't have to—"

"I'm perfectly capable—"

"I didn't say you weren't. But, sweetheart, I have the money and you're carrying our baby." He took a step closer. "Now can't you let me just take care of you? Just a little bit?"

Taking care of me was fine. It was the becoming used to it—relying on it—that I was afraid of.

But I'd decided to try this thing with Jordan and that meant pushing old fears away.

Even when it really, really scared me to do so.

I forced a smile. "You can." A pause. "Just a little bit."

He studied my expression, and I had the feeling that he understood exactly how much that acquiescence had cost me.

"Thank you." A brush of his lips against mine. "So tell me, where are the paper plates?"

"Second cupboard on the left. Forks are in the drawer next to the dishwasher."

He followed my directions and pulled out the plates and silverware, bringing both to the kitchen island, where I'd set up shop and was plucking fried wontons from a container I'd already opened.

"Oh, my God," I moaned. "This is the best thing I've ever had in my mouth."

"Setting yourself up there," he said.

"I'm surprised you resisted the innuendo," I teased.

"Me too."

I broke out into giggles, filling my plate with fried rice, chow mein, sweet and sour pork, and lots of wontons. "I almost commented on their salty deliciousness."

He smirked. "Now I wouldn't have been able to resist that one."

"Me neither."

We both laughed and sat down at the barstools, eating our fill.

"Dare I ask what you were taking issue with earlier?" Jordan ate a mouthful of rice. "Or should I let that sleeping dog lie?"

"You're brave," I said, having almost completely forgotten about the bags that were cluttering my counters. "But I'm fed now. I was protesting the fact that my kitchen looks like a drug store exploded inside of it."

"I need deodorant."

"Yes." I popped a wanton in my mouth. "That's a certainty."

"Smartass." He dropped his hand on my thigh.

"You know it."

A squeeze. "I do. But I'd like to not smell like a caveman while still being able to interact closely with you."

"You want me not to puke every time you're nearby."

"Well, yes, there's that."

"So"—I waved a hand at the bags littering my beautiful white marble—"drug store explosion?"

"No. Sniff test."

I groaned, dropping my forehead to the cold stone, before sitting up and glaring at him. "We should have conducted the *sniff test* before I had a full stomach."

Jordan set his fork down next to his plate and wiped his mouth with a napkin. I didn't have any of those unpacked either and figured it must have come alongside the food. "Damn. You're right. Sniff test will have to wait till tomorrow."

"Well, it'll have to at least wait until later," I told him. "Don't ruin Chinese food for me, okay?"

"I'll do my best."

"That's all I ask." I sat back in my barstool and patted my belly. "How did we eat so much food? I swear, I always have leftovers when I order in."

Jordan lifted one leg, placing it between both of mine. The action made my breath hitch and desire sweep through me, so much and so rapidly that I nearly missed the horrible joke that went along with the action. "Hollow leg."

"Oh my God," I said when I could speak without sounding like a breathless buffoon. "The dad jokes start already."

He huffed. "It wasn't *that* bad."

"Oh, but it was." I started giggling and Jordan joined in, his rumbling laughter making the leg between mine vibrate.

Now wasn't *that* nice?

"So no sniff test for the present," he said once I'd managed to pull myself together. "What should we do to pass the time?"

He waggled his brows mockingly, but the heat in his eyes belied the joking exterior. Jordan wanted me and I knew it.

"I've got a few ideas," I said, sliding from the stool then taking his hand in mine.

"This isn't what I had in mind," Jordan grumbled, sitting cross-legged next to me at my coffee table.

The coffee table.

Which looked ridiculously tiny with him sitting next to me.

Solid little thing. I couldn't believe we hadn't broken it that night.

And I wasn't supposed to be thinking about sex. Nope, that was the road that led to ruin and failing IUDs.

You can't get any more pregnant at the moment. The thought popped into my mind and I pushed it away.

Not the point.

This was our chance to take things slow.

"No complaining," I told him, picking up my crochet hook. "Crocheting helps my brain relax."

"If anyone ever saw me doing this—"

"You going to invite Heather over for a crochet party?" I asked.

"Fuck no."

"So, shh," I said. "And concentrate. Loop." I looped, showing him, trying not to laugh as he fumbled with the yarn. After a moment, he got it. "Pull the outside loop under the inside." I demonstrated. "And repeat."

He started to do it then mishandled the hook and the yarn slid off. A curse slipped from his lips.

"We can do something else," I offered. "Or you can just relax while—"

Blue eyes met mine and they were determined. "Show me again."

I did.

He followed my actions, tongue pressed into the corner of his lips as he concentrated fiercely. The yarn slipped off again. Another curse.

"Really—" I began.

A growl. "Again." His mouth softened. "Please."

I put down my hook and slipped between him and the table, forcing him to slide backward as I settled myself into his lap.

"This," he murmured, snaking his hands around my waist, "I like."

I shook my head, leaned back against his chest. "You need to relax," I told him, even as my actions made me do the opposite of my words.

Jordan's scent wrapped around me and that spicy maleness made me want to cuddle closer. That coupled with the heat of his body and the solidity of his muscles, and I was aroused beyond belief. I wanted to rub all over him, like he was catnip, curl up close and forget about the crocheting.

I wanted him. Maybe more than he wanted me.

But if I was doing this—making a go of the dating thing with Jordan—then I wasn't going to jump into bed with him again. That had been the crux of our problems, and I was determined to avoid that stumbling block this go around.

And dammit, the man was going to learn to crochet. It wasn't that hard.

I put the hook in his hand and placed mine over his. Then I did the same with the yarn.

"Loop. Tuck. Pull," I said and guided his hands through the actions. "Loop. Tuck. Pull."

He got it. Of course, the man got it. Two times through and perfect stitches, perfect tension. He repeated the action one more time. Two. Then he dropped the hook and yarn.

"That's good enough," he said, mouth coming close to my ear, his husky words making me shiver.

"There are other stitches—"

"I don't give a damn about the other stitches."

"Then what—?"

I didn't finish the sentence as Jordan spun me in his lap.

His mouth slammed down on mine.

And suddenly I didn't give a damn about the other stitches either.

TWENTY-TWO

Abby

I WAS ON FIRE. Oh God, I was on fire.

Jordan's hands were holding me tight against him, his lips plundering mine. It was too much and not enough. Our clothes were in the way. I wanted skin-to-skin. I wanted him on top of me.

And then with a shift of his mouth, everything changed.

The touch softened, his hands came up to gently cup my cheeks. His tongue was gentle and probing.

I sighed and he caught my breath.

"Hi," he said, pausing to stare down at me.

"H-hi." My heart was still pounding, that gnawing desire bubbling just under the surface.

His forehead dropped against mine. "You undo me."

I snorted. "Except you're not the one with wet panties right now."

He laughed, the sound puffing against my skin, filling my heart with a lightness that only seemed to appear when Jordan was nearby.

"True," he said. "Wet isn't really my problem at the moment."

My eyes drifted down and I smirked.

"No hammer jokes," he grumbled.

I couldn't help it. Apparently, I couldn't resist an innuendo.

"But there are so many good ones," I said, laughter punctuating the words. "It's—"

He kissed me again and it wasn't the hot, searing-me-to-the-soul kind. Nor was it gentle and coaxing. This one was demanding. He knew what he wanted from my mouth and he took it.

We broke apart, both breathing heavily.

I glared at him with heavy eyes. "Did you just kiss me to shut me up?"

"Did it work?" I opened my mouth indignantly, only to close it when he shot me a teasing look. "I kissed you because I can't seem to help myself." His lips twitched. "The shutting up part was just bonus."

I poked his chest. "Incorrigible."

"Your big words must come from all the books you read."

I fanned myself, fluttered my eyes. "Oh darling, you say the sweetest things."

"You *taste* sweet."

My breath caught. Jordan's hand stroked my waist, inching lower, slipping under the waistband of my slacks. "It's the fortune cookie."

"It's you." A dip of those fingers, calloused skin brushing the top of my underwear. "I bet you taste sweet here too."

"Jord—"

"Would you like it if I kissed you there?"

Now that was an image. Who wouldn't like Thor between her thighs? But . . . I'd been at work all day and wasn't sure how *fresh* I was.

"I—"

He tilted his head, fingers running back and forth, back and forth. I wanted them to dip a little deeper, to slide home. "You what?"

One lock of hair had slipped over his forehead and I brushed it back, feeling both extremely self-conscious and turned on. *He* smelled great. I, on the other hand, probably had B.O. and needed to douse myself in Purell.

"Sweetheart." He kissed my throat. "What is it? Do you want to go back to crocheting?"

The angst dissipated as I laughed. "God, no."

"Then what's the matter?"

"Just having a girl moment." I waved a hand. "Ignore me. I'll be fine in a minute."

His eyes narrowed and I sighed, knowing him well enough by now to understand he wouldn't let the point go without further explanation.

"I want you to go down on me, but I'm not sure how"—I waved a hand in the direction of my vagina—"good things are down there at the moment."

"Because of the baby?"

I shook my head. "It's been a long day. I haven't showered—"

Clarity finally dawned on his face. "You want me to eat you out but are worried about how you smell?"

I'm sure my cheeks were bright red. "Yup. That's pretty much the crux of it."

"Women."

"Hey! I'm trying to be considerate—"

"Shush, you." He picked me up, tossed me on the couch. "I'm trying to lick my girlfriend's pussy."

"Jord—" But my protest and embarrassment faded the moment he unzipped my pants and yanked them down my thighs. He dipped a finger beneath my underwear, eyes hot when he found me dripping.

All the air left my lungs when he put that finger in his mouth and sucked.

"Sweet," he said, voice gruff. "Like I said."

"Okay," I whispered in awe. "That might have been the hottest thing I've ever seen."

"No, that would be you writhing beneath me."

"But I—"

He didn't let me finish, instead yanked my pants past my ankles and started on my shirt. Something ripped. Buttons flew. My underwear disappeared like magic.

And in less time than I could have imagined, I was naked.

Jordan didn't give me a second to catch my breath. He spread my thighs, tossed one leg over his shoulder, and dove in.

"Oh my God," I moaned, and then hissed when he chuckled and the sound reverberated through me. He hadn't shaved for a few days, so his jaw was covered with stubble that added just the right amount of friction. If I'd been wet before, two seconds of his mouth on me and I was absolutely drenched.

His tongue circled my clit, flicking lightly for a few strokes before settling into the perfect rhythm. One warm palm slid up, cupped my breast.

"Oh," I moaned. "Just like that." My fingers tangled in his hair when he squeezed my nipple, teasing the hard nub as he licked me.

He switched breasts, sped the movement of his mouth until I was writhing against him. Both hands slid to my waist and he pulled me firmly against his lips, teasing, tormenting, winding me tighter and tighter and *tighter* until—

Explosion.

White stars flashed behind my closed lids. Pleasure spilled out from my center, radiating into my limbs and leaving me lax.

"Sweetheart?" Jordan's voice was gentle though laced with just a bit of stiffness. It brought me to my senses.

Slightly.

"Mmm," I said softly, words not having returned yet.

"Can you?" He shifted between my legs.

I sighed. "Hmm?"

"Can you let go?"

I blinked, trying to understand what he was talking about. "Killing my buzz, O'Keith."

Warm hands grasped mine, wrapping around my fingers and unlocking my fists. My eyes shot open to see my hands still wrapped in Jordan's hair.

And not gently.

I winced. "Sorry."

"I'm not." He grinned. "Hang tight." He rose and went into the kitchen.

A moment later he returned with a towel, wiped my thighs and in between.

"Beautiful," he murmured, kissing my cheeks. I knew they were red, but I ignored them.

"Not hardly," I said. "But thank you all the same."

"No arguments." He wiped his chin then sank down onto the couch and pulled me to his chest. "We've been through this all before, remember?"

"I remember," I said lazily, playing with a button on his shirt. "I also know what I look like. I'm fine. I like myself. But I'm not a supermodel."

"You're the most beautiful woman I've ever seen."

"And I'm going to accept that compliment, difficult though it may be." I yawned. "It's hard to undo years of Weasels with only one prince."

There was a moment of silence before I processed what I'd said.

"Not that *you're* a prince or—" I began.

Jordan laughed. "You think I'm a prince. No take-backsies."

"Oh lord," I groaned.

"Tell me more about these Weasels."

His hand was stroking my hair, petting me, making my eyes drift closed. The gentle caresses—and perhaps the best orgasm I'd ever had—loosened my lips.

"Oh," I said. "They're just jerks who sleep with me so they can get close to Seraphina." Another yawn. "We've gotten really good at picking them out."

"Hey." Warm fingers under my chin, tilting it back. I blinked my eyes open. "How many?"

"Many what?"

"Weasels." He clenched his jaw. "How many men have slept with you to get to her?"

I tugged my head free. "Does it matter?"

He dropped his hand to my arm. "Yes."

Well, he knew everything else about me. Might as well give him the last of it. "Three? Wait. No, *four*."

"Assholes."

I didn't deny the fact. "Good news is that we've gotten really good at detecting them." I lifted one shoulder. "Especially when you lose your virginity to one."

Jordan's nostrils flared. "And you thought I might be one?"

"I don't think you see yourself clearly," I said. "You're Thor reimagined. Tall and blond and all muscle-y. Put that with me—curvy, short, dark—and it doesn't make sense. Physically, anyway." My lips twisted. "*Physically* you're Seraphina's perfect match."

"I've never wanted her."

I smiled gently, running my hand down his chest. He was angry and tense, his words sharp. But not at me.

And I felt another part of my heart become enchanted with

the man next to me. Pieces were falling for him left and right and I knew that sooner or later I would be fully gone for him.

I might already be.

"You're in the minority," I said softly. "And that's okay," I added when he started to protest. "I'm comfortable in my own skin." A press of my lips to his cheek. "It helps that I've ensnared a god."

"What's with your obsession with Thor?"

"Have you *seen* Chris Hemsworth?"

"Of course."

"Abs. Chest. Arms. Hair." I tugged his lightly. "Grow yours out, and you'd give him a run for your money.

"Hilarious," he muttered.

"Regardless," I said, cuddling up against him. "You do it for me. And not just your body. I like the Jordan from the last few days very much."

"I like him too," he said, laughter in his voice.

"And modest too."

His chest rumbled and I let my eyes slide closed, enjoying the warmth of him, the feel of his fingers running through my hair. I sighed deeply.

He shifted, pulling free of my hold. I moaned in protest. At least until he picked me up from the couch and held me close. "Where's your bedroom?"

I wasn't sure I had the energy for a romp but decided I'd give it my best effort. After all, he'd graced me with the orgasm of all orgasms. "Upstairs. Last door on the right."

He carried me up, depositing me carefully beneath the comforter. I expected him to drop down on top of me. Instead, he asked, "Pajamas?"

I frowned. Was this some sort of kinky fantasy? Pajama fetish?

"You don't want to keep me naked?"

A masculine chuckle. "Believe me, you could stay naked for the rest of your life if you wanted." His lips touched mine. "But what do you normally sleep in?"

"A tank top and granny panties."

He smiled. "And where are said granny panties located?"

I was concentrating on the conversation, but between the post-orgasm glow and the fatigue seeping in, it was difficult. "In the closet. Top drawer on the far right. Tank tops are the drawer below. But what—?"

Without preamble, he spun and walked into my closet. My room was still in shambles, boxes piled against the walls. I'd gotten my clothes put away and the bed made, which was something. But just thinking about what was left to be unpacked made me break out into a cold sweat. The task seemed overwhelming.

Not that I was about to mention that to Jordan and encourage his highhandedness about the movers.

I might be relieved they were coming, but I wouldn't admit it. Nope, a girl had to have *some* pride.

A minute later, the man in question emerged with my jammies in his hand. He pulled the comforter back, slipped the tank top over my head, and tugged my underwear up and over my hips.

His eyes were scorching the whole time, his gaze scouring me from the inside out.

But he merely kissed my belly, tucked the blanket up under my chin, and then pressed his mouth to mine.

My head dropped to the side when he leaned back. His hammer was directly in view and he was packing a mega-sized version, not a compact. "Shouldn't we"—I indicated with my chin, since my arms were cozy warm under the comforter— "take care of that?"

He adjusted the waistband of his jeans and gave me a grin

that held a tinge of discomfort. "I think it's due a pass, don't you?"

I frowned. "Just because I didn't get off that night doesn't mean that I want to punish you now."

"I know," he said, but smiled to soften the words. "I want to take things slow with you, honey. And you're tired. Feeling you come against my mouth was enough."

I shifted to my side, glancing up at him and stifling a yawn. "When you say things like that I don't feel quite so tired."

Jordan kissed my cheek. "Go to sleep."

"Why not go for a quickie?" I asked. "There isn't any way I could come again this soon, but I'll enjoy it and that way, you'll get off too."

"I'm filing that statement away for future use," he said, cupping my cheek for a second before stepping back. "Plus, I don't want *anything* quick with you."

My eyes were drifting closed, but the words made me smile. "Jordan?"

"Hmm?" His voice sounded far away.

"What statement?"

"What?" he asked.

"What statement are you filing away?"

"Nothing, sweetheart. Sleep well." His footsteps were quiet on the carpet.

"Jordan?"

"What, baby?"

"Key on the counter in the kitchen." I yawned. "Take it. I don't need it."

"Okay, honey." He flicked off the lights. I heard the door start to close.

"Jordan?"

"Yes?" Even falling headlong into sleep, I could sense his amusement.

"Not quick sounds good to me, too."

TWENTY-THREE

Jordan

JORDAN STRETCHED and pushed back from his desk. His eyes were burning, but he and the team had finally managed a successful test run of the robot project.

"Have a name yet?"

He looked over his shoulder, a smile already on his face. It didn't matter what time of day it was, how long he'd been working, or who'd pissed him off. Abigail made him happy.

"No name yet," he said, crossing to where she stood leaning against the doorframe of his office.

Her chin tilted up and he kissed her, a soft touch that nonetheless had him going rock hard. He was a man starved . . . or maybe living on the edge. But he wasn't a man satisfied.

It had been two weeks since that night at Abby's house, and he could still taste her on his tongue.

But they'd both been swamped with work, and though he'd followed her home every night with dinner, he hadn't managed to carve out more time than that.

Hunter had been in the hospital and Jordan had tried to

spend every spare minute with his nephew. It was tough to see the vibrant little boy laid low, to see his body covered in wires and tubes. He was an innocent seven-year-old who had no one except Jordan, a mother who skipped town, and a nanny, who had spent more time with him than both of his parents combined.

Jordan honestly didn't know what he or Hunter would do without Cecilia. Luckily, though she was technically an employee, Cecilia seemed to love Hunter as her own.

As for George O'Keith, well, he might be paying the hospital bills, but he wasn't anything more than a checkbook.

Which had bugged Jordan at first. What was the point of opening his wallet if he wasn't going to spend time with Hunter? Jordan himself could afford the bills without strain, but his father had insisted to the point that he'd given in.

Then he'd understood.

It was too much like Mom.

His mother's illness and death hadn't been sudden. Cancer was a real asshole and it had chipped away at her body and soul, piece by piece. She'd wasted away, taking a part of all of them with her.

Hunter didn't have cancer.

Unfortunately, what he did have was congenital heart failure. He was weak, immunocompromised, and in desperate need of a transplant.

And neither Jordan nor George O'Keith could buy that for him.

Abby squeezed his arm, making him realize that he'd blanked out on her. "Are you okay?"

"I'm fine." He tugged her over to his desk chair and tapped her shoulder, guiding her down into it. "I was just trying to finish up everything because Hunter comes home today."

Her face brightened. She knew what was going on with

Hunter's illness and about the extended hospital stay. "Oh, that's great!"

"Yeah," he said, leaning against his desk in front of her. "So I'm going to have to cancel tonight."

"Of course," she said and though there was disappointment in her tone, her words were genuine. "Of course you have to. Hunter is way more important than a date night."

That was the moment it finally happened. The last piece was placed on the scale, finally tipping the balance and making him feel something he'd never thought possible—love.

Abigail hadn't met Hunter. The little boy wasn't anything more than a vague personality supported by pictures Jordan had shown her. And yet she was putting his nephew ahead of herself.

"You're important too," he said.

Her hand rested on his thigh. "He's an innocent little boy who's already been through too much. He needs you."

Jordan shoved a hand through his hair. "I hate that he has to deal with this bullshit. It's not fair."

Arms slid around his middle, held tight. "It is definitely not fair."

"I'm sorry to cancel," he murmured, slipping his arms around her in return and squeezing gently. "Though probably not as sorry as the rest of the team."

"What do you mean?" She leaned back, stared up at him.

"Sniff test being delayed again means that stinky Jordan is here to stay."

She laughed. "Is it better to be stinky or to be puke-causing?"

"I'm not sure."

Abby rose on tiptoe, pressing her nose to his neck and inhaling. "For what it's worth, I think you smell fabulous."

"Stinky turns you on?"

She grinned. "Apparently."

His cell phone buzzed and his eyes flicked down to where it sat screen up on his desk. The message was from Cecilia.

Heading home.

Abby touched his hand. "You'd better go."

"Yeah." Keeping one arm around her, he lifted the phone, sent back a response, then slipped it in his pocket. "But first I need to do this."

He kissed her, pouring all the desire he'd been banking for the last few weeks into it. All the frustration from finding his satisfaction with his hand, from waking up hard and aching. He poured *everything* into that kiss.

Including the love.

Eventually, they had to break apart and gasp for air. Abby dropped her head against his chest, breaths coming rapidly.

"You may . . . not . . . be able"—she sucked in a deep breath, steadying her words—"You may not be able to use that hammer, but your tongue is damn good."

He cupped her chin, pressed one more kiss to her mouth. "If I never hear another hammer innuendo, it will be too soon."

Another laugh, another shot of joy directly to his soul.

Damn, he loved this woman.

And somehow, that love grew even more when she paused in the doorway and said, "I think you should name the robot, Hunter."

A moment later, she was gone.

But she was the first one to give voice to the truth. He was pushing this project because of Hunter. Because his tech-savvy nephew not only wanted a robot he could play with from a hospital bed, but one that could also be taken apart and put back together again and again and again.

It was a simple request, but not an easy one. There wasn't anything on the market like that, so Jordan had decided to delay his beach plans to create one. Hunter had needed him.

But Hunter also needed it soon.

Because without a transplant, the doctors gave him six months.

TWENTY-FOUR

Abby

I SHOULD HAVE BEEN CONTENT, all curled up on the couch in a pair of cozy pajamas, a book in my lap, a cup of tea steaming on the coffee table.

My boxes were unpacked. My belly was full. My house wasn't half bad.

Okay, my house was awesome. I hadn't realized how much space I'd been lacking in my apartment until I'd upgraded and gotten over my guilt of using some of the trust fund money as a down payment.

My new, slightly better salary meant I could actually afford the mortgage, so I was considering the down payment my father's first gift to the baby.

Which he didn't know about yet.

I made a face and tried to focus on reading, a prospect that would typically suck me right in, especially since it was a good book from one of my favorite authors.

But I was restless for some reason.

Okay, not *some* reason. I was restless because I missed Jordan.

I peered out my front windows, saw that Seraphina's house was still dark. She'd invited me to a late dinner with her and Bec —who'd finally managed a few hours out of the office—but I hadn't felt like going.

Now I wished I had.

Because I was lonely.

How gross was that?

"Super gross," I muttered.

I placed my book across my knees and took a sip of tea, feeling it warm my body as I drank. After setting it down, I tried to pick up where I'd left off but only managed to reread the same paragraph three times.

My mind was wired, too pumped to focus, and I decided to save the book for a time when I could actually enjoy it.

"No sense in wasting a perfectly good alpha." I stuck in the old receipt I was using as a bookmark and set it on the arm of the couch before standing and walking into the kitchen.

I pulled my laptop from my case, settled into one of the barstools at the kitchen counter, and logged into the secure work server, deciding to get a bit ahead for Monday. I was just pulling up the folder I'd labeled *Project Hunter* when the doorbell rang.

"Hmm," I said, wondering who might be coming to the door at—I squinted at the clock—nine o'clock at night.

The bell rang again and I sighed, closing the laptop screen before sliding off the stool.

"Coming," I called as it chimed a third time. It cut off mid-ring.

I could feel the other person's impatience through the wooden panel as I approached and I knew that should have made me hurry. But I had this sinking sensation of who it might be.

He might be.

I'd been studiously avoiding his phone calls for the last couple of weeks and should have known better.

My father tilted his head to the side, face coming into view in one of the glass panels that bookended my front door. His hazel eyes were familiar—they matched my own—as was the fire shooting out of him.

I sighed. He must really be angry if he'd come himself.

"Here we go again," I said, glancing down at my stomach. I was in what I'd like to term the fat stage of the pregnancy. My butt and boobs seemed to have grown disproportionally, but my belly was still relatively flat, the little curve well-hidden beneath my loose pajama pants.

I unlocked the door and reached to open it, but my father beat me to it, pushing it open so quickly that I had to jump back to avoid being smacked in the face.

His bodyguard, Mac, trailed him closely, gaze searching my house for would-be assailants. Not finding any in the immediate vicinity, he smiled and winked at me.

I finger-waved. I'd always liked Mac.

"Hi, Dad," I said.

"Abigail." He strode right past me with barely a glance.

And the flash of eye contact I received was wholly dismissive.

I wished that dismissal still didn't cause a pang of hurt. I bit my lip. Unfortunately, it still did.

Ten seconds in my father's presence and I was a hurt little girl again.

I reached for the door to close it, but Mac beat me there. "Go ahead," he murmured, tone gentle. "I'll lock up."

"*Abigail*," my father said, impatience lacing each letter of my name.

And, shame on me, I hurried to him anyway.

I told myself it was because the sooner this was over with then the sooner he'd leave. I'd get back to my book or the project and—

But it wasn't about getting him to leave.

I wanted his approval. His pride.

My feet carried me to the kitchen, where my father stood stiffly, arms crossed fiercely over his chest, and I knew I wouldn't be getting either of those.

Nope. Fatherly appreciation wasn't in my future. Instead, a fight was heading my way.

I filled the kettle with water to stall the inevitable, setting it on the stove and turning on the gas.

"Tea?" I asked. "Or maybe coffee?" I opened a cupboard. "I think I have some somewhere."

"No."

"Okay." I reached for a fresh glass, not bothering with the one on the coffee table. I'd deal with that after The Reckoning. One tea bag in, then the hot water once it began steaming. While it steeped, I snagged the carton of milk from the fridge.

I didn't bother speaking to my father. His silence was typical. He used it with business associates—waiting them out, pushing them to crack.

I was accustomed to the tactic, so I kept myself busy making the perfect cup of tea.

It was either that or start blurting out all the reasons he might be mad at me.

And—peeking up at him as I poured milk into my tea— given the expression on his face, he didn't need any more ammunition for his fury.

He didn't speak as I put the cup on the island near my laptop. Nor as I returned the milk to the fridge. He didn't say a word as I walked by him and climbed back up into my stool.

Fine.

I opened my laptop, typed the information to log into the secure server again, and pulled up the design for the back of the packaging. It wasn't quite right yet.

I'd just started to adjust the shading when my father finally deemed it time to talk.

"Nice house."

Now *that* was a loaded two words, considering the last time I'd spoken to my father I had expressly told him to take his trust fund and shove it up his—

"Hmm," I replied, taking a page out of Heather's game plan.

I tried one filter before discarding it, not accomplishing much except to partially ignore my father.

Bernie Roberts wasn't a man easily ignored, and I was no different than the rest of America. Except that when it came to my father, I always had this pulsing hurt. Like a scraped knee exposed to the air. Stinging. Throbbing. Aching . . . for something different.

My eyes burned and I blinked rapidly to diffuse the waterworks. I was lucky. I was healthy, had a home and food. Mine was a life of privilege, and I wouldn't complain.

But sometimes a girl just wanted a hug from her dad.

The laptop screen closed, and I jerked my hands back to avoid my fingers being smashed.

I forced my eyes to my father's.

"What did you need, Dad?" I asked. "As you can see, I'm trying to get caught up on some work."

Fury darkened his gaze. "You're working for O'Keith."

My phone buzzed. I examined the screen, saw it was Jordan. Impeccable timing, that one. If my father saw his name—

Fireworks.

"I'm working for Heather O'Keith," I said, picking up my

cell and placing it in my lap. "Her tech company needed someone to oversee design and marketing."

"Why would they want *you*?"

Ouch. That one struck home and hard.

I forced my voice to remain calm. "Because, Dad, that's what my degree is in. That's what I spent the last six years doing with Robert and Susan before you bought up their business."

He leaned against the counter, position stiff and arrogant. His hair was still brown, not a hint of gray despite the fact that he was in his sixties. Wrinkles radiated out from the corners of his eyes and around his mouth.

Some might call them laugh lines.

I called them something different.

Asshole etching.

"I bought them out so you'd come to work for me."

Snorting, I took a sip of my tea and felt my phone buzz again. "Tell me, Dad," I said, placing the cup back down, "would the position at Roberts Enterprises involve real work?"

He scoffed. "Of course it would. Your brother needs help, someone to run his calendar. Make sure he doesn't miss lunch—"

"Doesn't he have an assistant for that?"

"I would have paid you better than an assistant," he said.

I allowed my eyes to travel around my kitchen, taking in the gray cabinets, marble countertops, top-of-the-line appliances. The rest of the house was the same. Wide moldings. Tall ceilings. Expensive flooring.

Yes, I was paying for it.

But only because my trust fund had given me enough of a head start to do so. And the fact that what I'd borrowed from it hadn't even made a dent should tell the world something. Should tell *my father* something.

Why would I need *more* money?

When had money ever given me something that wasn't strictly material?

I got it. I had privilege, had been born into it, never had to struggle, always had something to fall back on if I'd needed it.

But I also preferred to make my own way, on my own dime. And since I'd graduated from college, I had lived by that motto.

That I'd finally decided to cave and take a shortcut should have told my father something had changed.

He was just too wrapped up in himself to notice.

I sighed, slid from the stool, and gave my father a hug that he didn't return. "I love you," I said, pulling back. "But you would have never given me the opportunities I've found at RoboTech. I'm good at what I do. And, I'm sorry, but you missed out on that when you tried to shelf my abilities."

"Abigail, how dare—"

I closed my eyes. Breathed out deeply. Then I opened them and strode to the front door. "I'll see you in a few weeks at Christmas."

He sputtered as he followed me. "That's not the end of this conversation. You can't work for an O'Keith."

My brows came up. "I think I already am." I put one hand up, seeing the storm raging on his face. "And before you get into the trust fund talk—which by the way, you've pressured me to spend on a house for *years* now—I have something I need to tell you."

His jaw fell open, probably because I'd never taken that tone with him before. I'd never had a backbone when it came to my father.

Today, that changed.

"I'm pregnant." A pause as I sucked in a breath and decided to just say it and worry about the fireworks later.

His teeth clicked closed.

I lifted my chin. "By an O'Keith."

TWENTY-FIVE

Abby

ANY RESPONSE my father might have made was cut off by the sound of the doorbell ringing.

Good lord, my house was the revolving door tonight.

Mac slipped past us into the hall and started for it, only to step back and place his hand inside his jacket when the lock turned.

Oh shit.

Jordan.

My newfound courage slipped as he pushed open the door.

The only sign of his surprise at finding my father, me, and a bodyguard in the hall was a brief halt in motion. It was a millisecond, really, one I might have missed had I not been watching him so closely.

But I *was* watching, so I saw him take in the situation in an instant.

My father red-faced, skin mottled, smoke all but pouring out of his ears. Me, chewing on my lip, nerves starting to swell.

Mac, ready to reach for his gun.

I frowned at that. My father had kept a bodyguard with him for as long as I could remember, but I'd never really processed the fact that he might actually be in danger. Further that, I knew Mac had been with him for the last four or five years and I'd never seen him reach for a gun.

Well, I hadn't been around all that much, had I?

And now guilt was trickling in. Because how well did I really know my father? Was he truly in danger? Was I viewing him, perhaps unfairly, through the lens of my childhood?

Could he have changed?

Then I remembered our interaction in the kitchen and put the thought out of my head.

My father might have changed, but it wasn't a drastic difference, and it certainly hadn't changed the way he viewed me.

Bodyguard or not.

Jordan closed and locked the door behind him before striding casually toward us, stopping to shake Mac's hand as he walked by. "Haley," he said. "Good to see you."

Mac nodded then moved to stand in the corner, trying to give privacy to a situation that was impossible to ignore. Kind of hard when his charge was in the middle of it.

"Hey, sweetheart," Jordan said, stepping between my father and me, snaking a hand around my waist, and bending down to kiss me.

My father made a choking sound.

"Did you get my text?" he asked.

I shook my head, hands gripping his button-down tightly. He was still in his clothes from work, and I guessed he hadn't had the time to go home yet.

"No." I took in a breath, let his warmth and scent wash over me, steady me. I stepped back, tilted my head toward my father. "Jordan, this is my dad, Bernie."

"Good to see you again." Jordan put out his hand.

My father's remained at his side. "O'Keith."

Jordan raised his brows, turned toward me. "I finished early. Thought we might have our date after all."

"She's not dressed for it," my father burst out. "Obviously. So go."

Jordan's jaw tightened. "I'll have you know—"

"Jordan," I interrupted softly.

He looked down at me. I mouthed, "I got this."

His eyes searched mine for a long moment before he nodded. "Want a cup of tea?"

I smiled, not having realized that he'd noticed my addiction. I *should* have because he was thoughtful and considerate and always seemed to notice all the little details.

"Sure. Thanks."

He bent to kiss my cheek. "Holler if you need me," he whispered and headed into the kitchen.

"Him?" my father snapped. "You cannot be serious."

"Good to see you, Dad," I said, and walked to the front door. "I'll be over for Christmas as usual. Otherwise, if you want to discuss anything further, have your assistant call me and we'll coordinate calendars."

"That's it? You tell me you spread your legs for an O'Keith and you want me to coordinate calendars?"

"I'm twenty-seven years old," I said. "I don't need your permission for who I'm friends with, let alone who I sleep with."

"This is some convoluted revenge, isn't it? You think your childhood was so tough and now you're trying to deliberately—" Spittle flew as he ranted and I found the angrier he got, the calmer I felt.

"I didn't deliberately do anything. I'm just trying to live my life the only way I know how."

"This—" He shook his head. "I can't believe you—"

I let my head fall back to rest against the wall. I had hung two framed pictures of Bec, Sera, and me, centered above a console table that held a bowl for keys—my attempt at mending my losing ways.

"This is why I can't be around you," I said softly. "Everything is about you." I tipped my chin back down, met his eyes square on. "But *this* isn't and I suggest that if you want anything to do with your future grandbaby, then you stop judging me and let me live my own life."

"As if I'd want anything to do with a child that has O'Keith blood in it." He laughed, harsh and cold. "God knows if you are associating with *that* family, then you're as much of a whore as the rest of them."

The verbal blow took my breath away.

"Nice, Dad."

"You need to go." Jordan had come back into the hall and was standing very close to my father. Mac straightened from his position in the corner, but Jordan didn't do anything except say, "It's time for you to leave."

"Fuck you, asshole." Then my father punched him square in the jaw.

Jordan's head snapped back, his hands clenched into fists at his side. But he didn't even bother to address my father. Instead, he looked at Mac. "You need to get him out of here otherwise—"

"Coward."

The word drew Jordan's eyes down.

"I'll give you one freebie because she's your daughter and you're an old man." His voice went deadly. "But talk to her like that again and we're going to have a serious problem."

I stepped between them, leaned back against Jordan.

"Just go," I told my father.

Jordan was rock hard behind me and the fury radiating from him was almost a tangible thing. But when his arm wrapped around my waist, it was gentle.

Mac walked over and leaned down to whisper in my father's ear. My dad listened for a minute before turning disdainful eyes in my direction.

"I can't deal with this"—he sniffed at Jordan and me—"I have more important business to attend to."

Mac glanced at me and shook his head. I knew he'd made up whatever he'd told my father to diffuse the situation.

I nodded my thanks and locked the door behind them, collapsing back against it with a huge sigh. Tears were threatening but I didn't want to let them fall.

My dad was a jerk. No sense crying about it.

"Come here," Jordan said gruffly.

My eyes flashed open. He had his arms held wide and I didn't hesitate, just walked into that embrace.

"It's going to be okay," he whispered.

And even as I held the words close, I couldn't help but mentally shake my head at the irony.

I may not have gotten this comfort as a child, but I found that receiving it as a grown woman was just as good.

Actually, it may have been better.

"Why am I so nervous?" I asked Jordan the next morning as we drove to his father's house. He'd stayed for a little while the night before, long enough for me to heat up some leftovers for him and crochet a couple of rows on the baby blanket I'd decided to make for the nugget cooking in my belly.

He'd passed on the crocheting, opting to sit next to me watching the sports highlights as I'd worked.

The scene had been domestic and, scarily, I'd liked it.

He wanted to hang around longer, but I'd made him go home. The dark circles under his eyes spoke volumes. He needed more sleep, and that meant I couldn't monopolize all of his free time.

Even though I wanted to.

Even though I was quickly realizing that I wanted to spend every spare moment with him.

Even though I was as horny as a teenager.

"There's no reason to be nervous," he said, resting a hand on my thigh as he drove.

I mentally reset the conversation in my head and focused on the current task at hand. We were going to see Hunter, and I was freaking out.

I didn't do small children well. I was the youngest, had never been around little kids. And this one was sick. And special to Jordan. What if I said the wrong thing? What if—God forbid—I made Hunter cry? What if—?

"Why are you emotionally spiraling over there?" Jordan asked.

The question made me blink and squint over at him. Blue eyes flicked from the road to mine before returning forward.

"How—?"

"Sweetheart," he said, "I notice a lot of things about you."

"Scary," I muttered.

He squeezed my leg. "No hiding now," he said. "Not when I'm finally cluing in."

"That's what I'm afraid of," I said. But I felt the smile tugging at the corners of my lips.

"Spill."

"I'm scared Hunter won't like me."

"Sweetheart." His voice was gentle. "Just be yourself, and I guarantee he'll like you."

Aw.

"You think so?"

He winked. "I know so."

I blew out a breath and nodded. "Okay. I've got this."

"Yes, you do." His eyes met mine for a moment and there might have been a dash of nerves in the blue depths. "So," he said, tone far from confident, "I wanted to ask you something."

The thread of nervousness in his voice made me study him closely. "Go ahead," I said carefully.

"Do you want to go on a date?"

I cocked my head to the side, relief pouring through me. "Isn't that what we've been doing for the last few weeks now?"

"Well." He winced. "Sort of."

"We've spent almost every night together," I pointed out. "And had lunch. And"—I smiled—"you've brought me breakfast nearly every day. Now that I think about it, just about the only thing you do with me is try to shove food down my throat."

His cheeks went a little rosy. "It's important you eat. No more passing out."

"I agree." I put my hand over his. "And thank you," I said, joking aside. "I haven't felt dizzy since you started making me fat."

"It's nothing." His shoulders came up and I put my hand on the one I could reach, stopping the shrug in progress.

I didn't want him to dismiss what'd he'd done for me.

"It's not nothing to me," I said. "Thank you."

A moment of quiet then, "You're welcome."

"Okay, since we've established the whole spending-loads-of-time-together thing. Which I think is dating, isn't it?" I asked. "What's this about taking me out?"

"You deserve a nice dinner at a restaurant. Maybe a movie or a play. Flowers. Whatever." I didn't stop his shrug this time. "You deserve to be courted, Abs. We did this thing all ass-backward, I know. But I'd like to change that. Start from the beginning and have a do-over."

I laced my fingers with his. "I don't want a do-over," I told him. "I like where we are now. It's . . . easy? I'm not sure if that's the right word and maybe this is completely too soon and ridiculous or I'm addled with pregnancy hormones, but I feel like I know you better than any other person on the planet." I hesitated, biting my lip before I just decided to say it. "Maybe even better than Bec and Seraphina and I . . . I guess I kind of like it." I made a face. "No. That's a lie. I *really* like it."

Jordan was quiet for long enough to make me want to take what I'd said back. Then he turned his hand palm up and gripped mine tightly. "I really like it too."

I released a breath, feeling like we'd made a big promise that I didn't yet know the words to.

"Still, I wouldn't mind a nice dinner."

His laughter filled my heart. "Good," he said. "Tonight, I'm taking you on a date."

TWENTY-SIX

Abby

"JORDAN!" A tiny pair of arms wrapped tightly around Jordan's neck and I felt my eyes burn, my hand coming to rest protectively on my stomach.

"Sorry I missed you last night," Jordan said. "You were asleep by the time I got here."

"I'm always tired." Hunter's little freckled nose wrinkled. "It's annoying."

"Yeah," Jordan said, ruffling his hair and leaning back. "I bet it is. Hey, buddy. This is my friend, Abigail."

"Is she your girlfriend?" The wrinkle stayed in place.

Jordan looked solemn when he nodded.

"Ew. Girls are gross."

We both laughed as Cecilia, Hunter's nanny, came back into the room. "Hey," she said, putting her hands on her hips, her voice laced with mock-outrage. "*I'm* a girl."

"Well, that's okay because I love you, CeCe," Hunter said, and *I* promptly fell in love with *him*. "What's in your hand?"

It took me a minute to realize that Hunter was talking to me and then I examined the little bear I'd crocheted and felt embarrassment course through me. His room was jam-packed with stuffed animals and books, all of which looked a hell of a lot nicer than the lopsided bear with unevenly placed eyes I held.

"Oh," I said, turning it over in my hands. "It's silly, but when Jordan told me you were in the hospital, I-I made this for you."

Hunter tilted his head to the side. "Why?"

I nibbled on my lip. There was something about the fierce way his eyes focused on me that made me feel like a bug under a microscope. "I just thought you might be a little lonely and want something to cuddle." I resisted the urge to slide it behind my back. "It's not much, really."

"Can I have it?" he asked.

I nodded. "Of course."

I walked a little closer to the bed he was lying in. It was hospital grade, cleverly disguised with blankets and pillows to hide the institutional materials. But it was still a hospital bed, and that drove the seriousness of his situation home. I'd give this little kid anything he wanted.

He took the little green bear with the goofy eyes and studied it closely. "It's lumpy," he said.

"It's the first one I've made." I laughed. "I could use a little practice."

"First ones are special," he said solemnly, and hugged the bear. "It *is* cuddly."

"Good. At least I got *that* right."

Jordan was still sitting on the side of Hunter's bed and he tugged me down into his lap. "So tell me all about it, bud. What have you been doing this morning?"

"Causing trouble," Cecilia chimed in. She was sitting on the floor folding laundry.

Jordan raised his brows and Hunter stubbornly put out his bottom lip. "I wanted to play with my aunts and uncles."

It took me a minute to comprehend that Hunter meant Jordan's half-siblings, who currently lived in the house. From what I knew, they were all around Hunter's age and would have been perfect built-in friends.

"He wanted to play *football* with his uncles and aunts."

Jordan hissed out a breath.

"I miss running," Hunter said, and crossed his arms. "It's not fair."

"I know, buddy." The anguish in Jordan's tone killed me. "I wish that I could make this go away for you. But—"

"You can't." A sigh. "I know."

"I've got an idea," I said, turning to Cecilia. "Can Hunter go outside?"

"He can *sit* outside."

"No running. No jumping. No playing. No fun," Hunter grumbled.

I stood and tugged Jordan's arm. "Give us twenty minutes," I said, "and I'll see what I can do about the fun part."

"Ready, Hunter?" I asked, adjusting Jordan's shoulders so that he was standing straight.

He giggled. "This is going to go really bad."

"Yes, it is," grumbled Jordan.

Which only made Hunter laugh harder.

Cecilia tucked the blanket tighter around his shoulders then sat down in the empty chair next to his.

Chairs weren't the only things we'd brought out onto the patio, but I had used a lot of them in my plan. And rope. And potted plants. And . . . a blindfold.

That was currently wrapped around Jordan's eyes.

"Okay, remember what to do? You tell Uncle Jordan what direction to walk and when to stop and try to get him through the whole obstacle course without running into anything."

Hunter nodded, his smile huge.

"Try not to make me fall off a cliff," Jordan said.

Hunter broke out into peals of laughter.

"The pool's not too far," I stage-whispered and Jordan growled, making Cecilia and me join in with Hunter's amusement.

"I fall in," Jordan said, "and I'm taking you with me."

"You'd have to catch me first."

His arm snaked out and caught my wrist. He tugged me into his arms and pressed a kiss to my mouth, aim true despite the blindfold. "I always know where you are, sweetheart."

"Abby-dar?" I said, my heart pounding in my chest.

He released me, fingers brushing the sides of my breasts as he set me away from him.

"Jordan," I hissed, "Hunter is right there."

"They're not paying attention."

I glanced over my shoulder to where Hunter and Cecilia sat. Jordan was right, they were in heated debate, the words "pool," "uncle," and "no" featured loudly.

"How would you know that they're not—" I gasped, spotted one blue eye peeking beneath the blindfold. "You're such a cheater."

He grinned. "A man's got to do what a man's got to do." He swatted my butt, pretended to stretch and then said louder, "Okay, bud, time to stop plotting. Should we do this?"

"Yes!" Hunter yelled, eyes mischievous.

"Wait!" I grabbed Jordan's arm and fixed the blindfold. "No cheating."

"Woman—"

"Walk forward," Hunter commanded.

I bit back my smile as Jordan took a step forward and promptly walked into a rope, knocking several chairs out of alignment.

"Sorry," Hunter said, maybe a little too cheerfully.

"Hang on," I told Jordan, and righted the chairs, then took his shoulders and aimed him in the proper direction of the course's start.

"You're doing this next," I called. "So you'd better be nice to your uncle."

Hunter's mouth made a little "o" and just that quickly, he got serious about helping Jordan through the course.

"Walk forward. Stop." He turned to Cecilia and held up a palm. "What hand is this?"

She whispered the answer.

"Go right!" he yelled.

"*His* right," I said to Jordan, who turned left and managed to avoid the potted plant blocking the other path.

"Now crawl," Hunter ordered.

Jordan dropped and attempted to squeeze through the cardboard box we'd found in the garage.

The sight of Thor on his hands and knees getting stuck in the tiny hole I'd cut out of the side of the box was too much for me. I started chuckling and couldn't stop. Not when he managed to struggle through, not when Hunter told him to go left and he knocked over a plant, not even when he managed to get wrapped in the duct tape I'd strung between two chairs.

"Which left?" he called, covered in silver stripes like a metal mummy. He was bent over, trying to remove the pieces from his ankles and his voice was desperate. "Mine or his? *Mine or his?*"

"His," Cecilia and I managed to get out while still chuckling.

Two more turns, one more crawl, and Jordan was free of the maze. He took his blindfold off and glared at me then Cecilia.

"This is not that funny!"

I held my stomach as I giggled. "My abs. Oh my God, laughing through that was the hardest workout I've had in months."

Cecilia rubbed her cheeks. "Even my face hurts."

"You're in so much trouble," he said and though he was looking at Hunter, I knew the words were directed at me.

"You can make it up to me later," I joked.

He turned to me, eyes sharp. "You'd better count on it."

"Sniff it," Jordan ordered.

"Uh-uh," I said, shaking my head and turning my face away. "The last one was bad enough."

My stomach was *still* queasy. I'd smelled twenty-something deodorants at this point and they were all bad.

All of them.

"This is the last one," he said, offering it up to me like it was a piece of broccoli and I was a finicky toddler. "Smell it, and I promise this is the end."

"Promise?" I raised my eyes to his and when he nodded, I sighed in resignation. "Fine." I carefully took the deodorant from his hand and removed the lid. I brought it about a foot from my nose and took a cautious sniff.

Blegh.

I capped it and shook my head, dropping it to the counter and backing away.

"Damn," he said. "That was supposed to be the unscented stuff."

"Well, it's not unscented to me."

He dropped it into the trash can then removed the bag and walked through the garage to throw the offending deodorants into the outside garbage bin. A minute later, he was back. "What type do you use?"

I was wiping my nose on a tissue, trying to somehow remove the scent from my nostrils. "Of deodorant?" I asked, slightly nasally.

"Yeah."

I told him.

"Do you mind if we try it?"

"You want to put on my deodorant?" I asked.

"Want is the wrong word. I'd like to be able to not stink my office up and also not make you sick. What you're wearing doesn't make you puke, right?" He shrugged. "Seems worth a try."

I stood up and inclined my head in the direction of my bedroom. "Seems like we should have given it a try before you made me smell all of those other gross ones."

"At least we did it before dinner?"

I groaned, stomach feeling a bit raw. "Don't mention food right now."

"Sorry." He pressed close to my spine. "I'm trying to help."

"I know." I turned in his arms and hugged him. "Thank you."

Hands slid down my back, cupped my hips. I wanted them to slide lower, to keep going and cup something else.

Unfortunately, Jordan released me, taking my hand and tugging me up the stairs.

"Jordan?" I asked as we walked through my bedroom door and headed for my bathroom. "Is there a reason you haven't fucked me again?"

His fingers spasmed on mine. "What?" He turned to face me.

"I-I just—you haven't seemed interested." I shrugged, dropped my eyes. "You've held me and we kissed a few times. But it's mostly—" I broke off.

"Mostly what?"

I grimaced. "Well, friendly."

"You think I feel *friendly* about you?"

"I mean, I guess not. I just— We haven't— Not since that night you—" I pointed south. "It's okay. I just . . ."

Was making a royal mess of this.

"I've jerked off to the image of you coming against my mouth every night for the last three weeks." His stare bored into me. "I've imagined the taste and heat of you. I've pictured myself inside of you." He grabbed my hand, placed it on his . . . hammer, which was hard enough to pound nails.

Or maybe pound something—*someone*—else.

"I want you, Abigail. Don't you ever doubt that."

"Then why haven't you—?"

"I was trying to give us time to get to know each other. We both have a lot of outside pressure right now. I didn't want to add to it."

"I don't think giving me mind-blowing orgasms is a bad type of pressure."

One brow rose. "Mind-blowing?"

"Oh yeah," I said. "I thought you were well on your way to redeeming you and your *hammer* skills. Then you backed off."

I waited to see if he'd deny it.

He didn't.

Instead, his expression went thoughtful. He nodded. "I did back off. I think . . . I think that things have been so intense between us that I gave distance when I should have closed it. You're not like any other woman I've ever met, Abby. You've got me so twisted up that I don't know how to move forward."

"I—"

"It's not a bad thing. Just unfamiliar ground to navigate." He cupped my cheek. "Like how you were with Hunter today—that killed me. You were so perfect, so sweet. Then I think about you with our baby, and I just get lost in this fantasy." A sigh. "And then I remember we went from step A to step Z skipping everything in between and I keep thinking I owe it to you to give you B through Y. It's almost paralyzing."

"I don't need B through Y," I said. "I just want to be with you. I want to know everything about you. I want to watch bad movies and crochet with you and not put any expectations on anything."

"I'm not used to having no expectations."

I couldn't have expectations, not when every person in my life aside from Seraphina and Bec had completely obliterated the ones I'd had for them. I couldn't expect perfection and happy endings, not when what I was developing with Jordan already meant so much.

If I started dreaming of the other end of the rainbow, of picket fences and family holidays, I thought I might be thoroughly decimated when we were through.

"I know," I said. "But can we try? Can we keep moving forward without all the pressure of worrying about whether or not we're doing it right?"

He nodded.

"Thank you." I rose on tiptoe to touch my lips to his.

Jordan's expression altered, turning a little hotter, slightly playful. "So no planning, right?"

"Right. We just live in the moment and—*oof!*"

He jerked me to his chest. "Shh. For now, we're going to live."

And then he lowered his head to mine.

TWENTY-SEVEN

Jordan

ABIGAIL in his arms was the best thing in the world. She was soft and warm and smelled like roses, and when she moaned against his lips, pressing harder against his chest, Jordan's arousal went from hanging on by a thread to roaring out of control.

He put his hands on her shoulders, tugging her back.

"But—"

One move and she was in his arms. He carried her to the bed, ripped back the comforter, then set her on the sheets.

Pink cheeks, swollen lips, mussed hair. She would have said it was crazy, that her locks were out of control, but he thought the way they were spread out across her pillow was the sexiest thing he'd ever seen.

"Hi," he whispered, coming down beside her on the mattress.

Her mouth quirked up. "Hi."

"You're so beautiful." A roll of her eyes—another dismissal that was so typically Abby. He gripped her chin, forced her to look at him. "I gave you no expectations, so you need to give me this. You are the most beautiful woman inside"—he pressed his palm to her heart, felt the rapid *thump-thump* of her pulse— "and out."

"Jordan." She sighed, covering his hand with her own. "What am I supposed to do with that?"

"Accept it."

A snort.

"Now shh." He kissed her before she could protest further, slipping his tongue into her mouth and coaxing hers to join in. The heat, the *spark* he felt at just the press of their mouths was insane. His entire body felt on the edge of implosion, just from one kiss.

Her hands threaded through his hair, gripping tightly, and the slight bit of discomfort propelled him headlong over the edge.

He found the waistband of her pajama pants, shoved them down, then tore his mouth free from hers to pull off her shirt.

In less than ten seconds, she was naked except for a tiny pair of blue panties. Pale skin flushed pink, breasts stiff-peaked and waiting for his mouth, the slightest hint of her arousal soaking through her cotton underwear.

His mouth watered.

Slowly, wanting to savor the moment, to make it better for her than their first encounter, Jordan traced his hands up her waist.

Gooseflesh erupted on her skin, and she hissed out a breath. "That tickles."

"Mmm," he said, bending so that his mouth could follow the same path. Her waist, her stomach, and then up . . . up until he reached her breasts. He rubbed his nose against the underside of one, before leaning back slightly to blow on her nipple. "I read they can be extra sensitive. Is this okay?"

"Uh-huh." She arched back, pressing her breast closer. "I want—"

He licked the hardened nub, relished her moan. "What do you want, sweetheart?"

"I—" Hands came up to his head again and tugged him back down. "They're—" Another swipe of his tongue. "Not . . . *ah* . . . sensitive. I want—" She pulled his head toward her breast and groaned when he held steady, staring into those gorgeous, lust-filled hazel eyes. "You. Jordan. I need your mouth."

He'd wanted the words, *needed* them, but they nearly shattered what remained of his tattered control. He wanted to make this perfect.

And it meant more to him than his own pleasure.

It meant more to him than anything else did in that moment. More than the company, the robot project, the beach.

The only thing that mattered was pleasuring Abby.

He closed his mouth around her nipple and gave her everything he had, every skill he'd honed, every tactic he knew. Jordan paid more attention to her responses than any other woman from his past, noting every moan, every hitch of breath. He exploited the information, using it to discover what set her on fire.

From her breasts, he moved up to her mouth, feasted on her throat, and then kissed his way down her body.

There was a soft curve just below her belly button and his heart squeezed, his desire banking for a moment as he glanced up and met Abby's eyes. He saw in them what he felt in his heart. Hope, fear, and love.

He felt love for the baby and . . . for Abigail.

Carefully, he pressed his lips to the little bump. He was in love with Abby.

Holy shit, he was *in love*.

Shaking fingers touched his cheek. "Jordan?"

"I know, sweetheart," he said. "I know."

It was like one of those moments in a movie, where the main characters stare at each other and a montage of their past interactions start playing. Except this was real life and the moments were a blur, the huge feelings he felt for this women so much more.

"I need you." One shift of her hips and the time for emotion was over.

He slid lower, spread her legs, and began feasting.

Fuck, she tasted amazing. Sweet with just a hint of tart, it was the best meal of his life.

"Oh, God," Abby moaned, hips writhing. "That's"—he slid one finger home—"oh, fuck. *Jordan.*"

Another finger and he moaned at the tight fit, remembering what she'd feel like, imagining himself sliding home. His slacks were uncomfortably tight and he was slowly dying from the need to be inside her.

"I—" She gasped. "That's—" Her head rolled from side to side on the pillow, her hips bucked against his mouth. "Oh . . . *fuuuck.*"

She pulsed against his finger, squeezing him tightly as her orgasm pulled her over the edge.

Her chest rose and fell, breasts jiggling, a sheen of sweat coating her skin. Her pussy was pink and glistening, and he had to force his eyes to the ceiling and count backward from one hundred to not blow his load.

"Jordan?" she asked after a minute.

"Yeah?" He was still counting.

"Why aren't you inside me?"

His head jerked. "What?"

She sat up, hands finding the buttons on his shirt and sliding one free. Then the next and the next and the next. He shoved it off when they were all loose. The buttons on the cuffs caught on his wrists and he yanked them through, not giving a damn when he heard the fabric rip.

Because Abby's hands hadn't stopped.

They'd continued to unbutton his slacks and then had progressed to zipper sliding.

Hot palms on his chest, his stomach, beneath his boxer briefs and—

"Oh fuck," he groaned when she gripped him tightly.

"There you are," she whispered, but she wasn't talking to him. No, the words were for his *hammer*—fuck, now *he* was the one making hammer references—and the way she licked her lips nearly made him come right then and there.

Which made alarm bells blare in his head.

"Next time," he said, extracting himself from her hands and bending to kiss her. He thrust his tongue past her lips and slipped his fingers back between her thighs. She jumped then moaned when he gentled the strokes, knowing that she was still sensitive.

Abby was so responsive that he wanted to spend the night making her come over and over again.

He wanted to claim her, body and soul. To mark her from the inside out. To tattoo her heart with his name.

To tie her to him for an eternity.

But most of all, in that moment, he couldn't wait another second to be *in* her.

He kicked out of his slacks and knelt between her thighs.

I love you, he thought, and thrust home.

TWENTY-EIGHT

Abby

I REALLY LOVED *this man's hammer,* I thought, gasping as Jordan slid inside me with one firm stroke. It was too much yet not enough. Well, not the hammer part—*that* was great—but the rest of it.

What we were sharing wasn't just physical. It was more.

And that scared me.

I wanted to keep emotions out of it, but I couldn't.

Every time we were together, whether it was sexual or not—and more often it had been *not*—I felt another thread connect us.

Or, rather, I felt another string attach *me* to *him.*

And I worried about what might happen when he inevitably severed the ties.

Because it would have to come from him. I was too addicted to his particular brand of perfect to distance myself now. I'd jumped in with both feet and prayed that he wouldn't find me lacking—

Which was seriously fucked up, I realized.

My worth shouldn't come from another person. But it had somehow become interlaced with his . . . what? Acceptance? Thoughtfulness? Approval?

Oh, my God. I was *so* fucked up. How was I going to raise this baby without screwing him or her up? How—?

"Abigail."

Jordan was on top of me, *inside me,* and I was having a panic attack. "It's not you," I said. "It's—oh, God"—my hands came up, covered my face—"*oh, God.* I'm ruining this. I'm sorry. I'm so sorry."

I was hiccupping now, sobs escaping my chest, tears leaking, and I didn't completely understand why except that when he'd slid inside me it had felt so perfect and I knew perfect couldn't last. I just knew I'd do something to fuck it up.

And now I was. I was screwing it all up.

"Sweetheart." He tugged at my hands, but I shook my head. I was embarrassed enough, he didn't need to see my snot-covered, splotchy face.

Because I wasn't crying pretty.

This wasn't one perfect tear sliding down my cheek, like a romance novel. These weren't tears symbolizing the fruition of a relationship and hope for the future.

These were frightened sobs from a woman who felt too much.

This was me being unable to take that final leap and just put it all on the line.

This was—

"I love you."

I froze, sobs sticking in my chest. My arms went lax and Jordan gently peeled them from my face. He leaned close, close enough that I could see the specks of gray-green lining the deep blue of his irises.

Beautiful.

"Abigail Roberts," he said, one palm cupping my cheek. "I. Love. You."

It scared me, those words. But it scared me more to do this without them.

Because . . .

"I love you too."

He shuddered, reminding me that he was still hard, still deep inside.

"I like hearing you say that," he murmured, resting his forehead on mine.

Serenity swept through me in that moment, erasing the fear, eradicating those persistent doubts.

There were just the two of us in this bed. The rest of the world could wait.

Calmness reigned . . . but just for a minute.

"Okay?" he asked.

I nodded. "Sorry I freaked out."

"If you're feeling what I'm feeling then I say we're due a freak out every once in a while."

"When are you going to freak out?" I asked, pushing back a strand of hair.

"Probably not when I'm inside your heat and dying to move." He gave me a pained look. "You feel incredible."

"I know." I smiled, before tugging his mouth down to mine. "Now move."

He didn't need to be told twice.

THE PHONE CALL came eleven days before Christmas, while Jordan sat next to me in Dr. Stephens' exam room. She measured the baby's growth and it was crazy to see the difference that just a month had made.

Fourteen weeks since that bad night stand.

Fourteen times seven—it was too early in the morning to do the math—days since my life had taken a sharp left.

Jordan had all but moved into my house, even going so far as to sneakily claim a drawer and buy an extra tube of my deodorant to leave on my bathroom counter. And though we worked long hours and we spent a lot of time with Hunter, we were managing to carve out time for just the two of us.

Time that I relished.

Time that I loved—even if it was just streaming a bad TV show and eating takeout, even if it was just working opposite one another on my kitchen island, laptops dueling.

Even if it was crocheting together and making fun of the garish and mismatched colors he'd chosen for the scarf/blanket/lumpy-square-handkerchief.

I didn't want to share him with the world.

But I wasn't the only one who needed him.

So when Jordan's cell rang and he turned it to silent instead of answering it, I touched his hand. "That's Hunter's ringtone."

"It's—"

I shook my head. "Answer it. What if he's—?"

Sick. Hurt. In the hospital. Lonely and all by himself.

He studied me for a second before pulling out his cell and excusing himself to the corner of the room.

"His nephew," I told Dr. Stephens. "He's in need of a heart transplant."

Her eyes dimmed. "How old?"

"Seven," I said softly. "Mom bailed. Dad passed away."

"Damn," she said, peeling off her gloves and patting my knee. I slid up, tucked the drape back over myself. "It's always so much worse when it's kids."

I nodded. "I agree completely. He's the best kid, too. Smart and precocious—"

"He got it," Jordan said, his face blank. "I—*he got it.*"

"Got what?" Dr. Stephens asked.

"A heart." Jordan's voice was stunned. "Hunter is on the way here with Cecilia. They have a heart for him."

"Oh, my God." I started to stand, remembered I was bottomless and froze.

Dr. Stephens squeezed my hand. "You're all set here. I hope everything goes okay. Call me if you need anything."

"Thank you," I said.

She left, closing the door behind her.

"Jordan," I said. "He'll be okay. It's—"

"I want to get custody of him," he said. "Once this is all said and done. I don't want him alone. I want him with me." His eyes met mine. "With us."

My breath caught. "I—I—"

I breathed in then out, very slowly. I wanted that too. So much. I already loved Hunter like my own.

"We'll get him through this," I said, knowing that he had a fight ahead of him. "Then we'll figure out what Hunter wants." I wouldn't take him from Cecilia, the one other solid in his life. If—no, *when*—Hunter was healthy and strong, we'd figure it out.

And it would involve Jordan and me.

I couldn't let that little boy grow up without us.

WE MET Cecilia and Hunter in the waiting room of the transplant center.

"Did you grab the papers?" Jordan asked.

"I did." Cecilia handed a folder over and Jordan flipped through it, sighing when he reached a page.

"Good," he said, pulling two legal documents out, glancing

quickly at both, then sticking them back inside. "Everything is here."

"Want me to hold that?" I asked, leaning up to whisper in his ear. "Hunter looks like he could use a little Uncle Jordan time."

We both glanced over at the little boy, whose typically pale skin was even paler than normal. Jordan handed me the folder then bent to pick up Hunter. "All ready, buddy?"

Hunter's bottom lip trembled. "Uh-uh."

One big palm wrapped around the back of Hunter's neck and pulled him against Jordan's chest. He bent his head, speaking softly into Hunter's ear. I couldn't hear the words he whispered, but I saw the effect: a gradual relaxing, a growing confidence, and finally two little arms being thrown around his uncle's neck.

Cecilia sniffed and I wiped a finger under each eye.

"Sometimes I wish that Jordan was Hunter's dad," the younger woman said.

"I think he wishes that too," I told her.

"Do you think—?" she broke off. "Never mind. We need to think about the surgery right now."

"Would you mind if he—if *we* . . . someday?"

It was barely a coherent sentence, but Cecilia understood me anyway.

Her lips pressed tightly together. "I would love it if Hunter found his own family." She stared at me, fury in her eyes. "She signed away her rights, you know?" A nod in the direction of the folder.

"What?" I opened the cardstock cover and my heart sank. "How could . . .?"

"I know." Cecilia touched my arm. "And I know that you have a lot happening." Her eyes drifted down to my stomach even though neither Jordan nor I had mentioned the baby to her or Hunter. Hell, as far as I knew, he hadn't even told his father.

Heather knew, of course, because of the whole sleeping-on-day-one-of-my-new-job situation. Yet she hadn't mentioned it to me.

But Cecilia, a woman who barely knew me, had picked up on it.

She smiled. "I'd love it if you two could take Hunter. He worships Jordan and he adores you. He deserves more—" She shook her head. "He deserves more than just a nanny."

"Hey." I turned to face her fully and though I wasn't the most touchy-feely person, especially with people I didn't know all that well, I hugged Cecilia tightly. We hadn't spent years together, but I felt like I knew her heart.

And that heart was pure.

"Hunter is lucky to have you."

She sniffed and pulled back, glancing up at the ceiling and blinking rapidly. "I'm scared," she said softly. "I shouldn't be. I need to be strong for him. But I'm petrified."

"Me too," I admitted. "But we're going to pretend otherwise. Deal?"

Cecilia nodded, blew out a long, slow breath. "Deal."

"And," I said, as a few nurses pushed through the double doors and began walking toward our little group, "when Hunter becomes an official part of our family, I hope you will too."

Her jaw dropped open and she looked at me, dumbstruck. But she didn't get a chance to respond because Hunter ran over, grabbed both of our hands, and began tugging us forward.

"Come on, CeCe and Abby. Today I get to become a superhero!"

TWENTY-NINE

Abby

"I CHECKED OVER THE ORGAN MYSELF," the lead doctor said. "Everything looks perfect so we'll begin prepping Hunter for the surgery and get him feeling better."

Hunter was in bed, his little body dwarfed by a white hospital gown covered with pouncing tigers.

The image fit him.

Launching himself forward for a chance at the future.

"Do you think my new heart will be working by tomorrow?" Hunter asked. "Because I'd like to have it in time for me to turn eight."

"Is it your birthday tomorrow?" the nurse asked, placing a blood pressure cuff on his upper arm.

"Uh-huh," he said around the thermometer.

"Well, if the doctor okays it tomorrow, I'll save you a celebratory Jell-O." She noted a few items on the chart.

"I love Jell-O!"

"Great!" She fist bumped him. "What's your favorite flavor?"

"Cherry!"

"Done," she said. "I'm going to mark one in the fridge with your name on it right now."

"Yay!" Hunter bounced on the bed. "That's awesome."

"What do you say?" Cecilia prompted.

"Thank you!" Hunter called as the nurse moved toward the door.

She smiled, waving her goodbye.

The doctor walked over to Hunter and began talking to him, explaining what was going to happen in vague, kid-friendly terms. Ten minutes later, and after answering about a hundred questions from Hunter, he left with a promise that the anesthesiologist would be in soon.

I watched from the corner as Jordan and Cecilia sat and joked with Hunter, not wanting to intrude.

I probably should have gone to the waiting room, but I didn't want to take my eyes off Hunter until the last possible moment.

And when he asked me to come over and hold his hand so the nurse could start his IV, I knew that little boy owned me, whether he was aware of it or not. His whimpers of pain, the tears in his eyes, all of them slayed me.

Thankfully, the procedure was quick and within minutes, the anesthesiologist was in the room, giving Hunter a medication that made him drowsy.

A few moments later he was being wheeled away, a piece of my heart rolling alongside him.

"How is he?" Heather asked from the doorway of my office the next afternoon.

I winced. "In some pain," I said, honestly. Watching him

hurt was probably the worst thing I'd experienced in my life to date. "But the doctors said that everything went perfectly."

She came in and closed the door. "Did you want to take some time off to be with him?"

My eyes flew up, surprised.

"You've been a mess today. Unfocused. Out of sorts."

My stomach clenched. "I'm sorry. I'll make sure I don't—"

"That's not what I meant," she said. "I get it. I'm worried too, and the kid isn't mine."

I shook my head. "It's not like that. Hunter's not my—I mean it's just . . . you don't have to—"

"Abby." She smiled. "Hunter is Jordan's, and Jordan is yours. So Hunter is yours."

"Is this some sort of if X equals Y and Y equals Z then X equals Z nonsense?"

She groaned, dropping into a chair in front of my desk. "Stop. You're bringing back horrible memories of algebra class."

"You're incredible with numbers," I reminded her.

"Yes. With real numbers. It's the alphanumeric ones that get me every time."

I laughed then sobered. "I want to be with Hunter, but I also want to make sure I do this project right. It means so much to Jordan. I don't want to be the one who—"

"Screws it up?" Heather asked, rather unhelpfully if you asked me.

"Yes. That," I said, grimacing.

"So keep working," she said. "Just do it remotely."

"What?"

Heather rolled her eyes. "You're already doing it anyway." Her brows went up at my expression. "Don't think I've haven't seen how frequently you log in to the server from home. Plus, that's going to be how you work when the baby gets here, isn't it? Think of it as a trial run."

"Wait, what?" I asked.

"You are going to keep working here after the baby, aren't you?"

"Y-yes," I stumbled out. "I mean I'd planned to, I just hadn't thought that far ahead and—"

"Good. I'll plan it for you." Heather grinned. "I kind of like doing that, if you hadn't noticed."

I snorted. "Yeah. I think I managed to pick up on that."

"Okay, great. It's settled then. Pack up and get out of here." She stood. "I don't want to see you until Hunter is home from the hospital."

"Heather?" I asked as she turned to the door.

She stopped, rotating back to face me.

"Thanks."

Her lips twitched and she shrugged. "Don't know if you know this, kid, but I kind of like you."

"Somehow I like you too." She laughed and started out again.

I stopped her. Again.

Because something she'd said had triggered alarm bells in my mind.

"Before you go, can you tell me how often, exactly, I've been logging into the secure server?"

THIRTY

Jordan

JORDAN READ the press release with a mixture of growing horror and extreme fury.

This is why he'd gotten rid of his cell phone in the first place.

What he'd thought was going to be an innocent—or very naughty, he liked both options—text message from the woman he loved had turned into something far more sinister.

He glanced over at the hospital bed where Hunter slept. It had been a week since the surgery, a week of seeing Hunter for small slices of time, of trading places with Cecilia and Abby so that one of them was always in the waiting room in case Hunter might need them. In fact, Abby had spent so much time in the waiting room that she had her own desk. Or rather, the nurses had encouraged her to rearrange a table and chair next to a plug so she could work remotely.

And now he wondered what exactly she'd been working on.

Fuck. Jordan sucked in a breath, blew it out slowly, and focused on Hunter. This wasn't about work or betrayals. This was about a little boy who had spent most of the past week sedated or sleeping. He'd been moved from the cardiac intensive care unit to a room in the general cardiac ward the night before. Though it was an improvement, his nephew still had a long journey ahead of him.

A soft knock on the door drew his attention from Hunter. He tore his gaze away and saw the nurse who was on shift, Rebecca, standing in the door. "I'm sorry," she murmured. "Visiting hours are over."

"Okay." He crossed to Hunter, pressed a kiss to his forehead. "'Night, buddy."

His nephew stirred slightly but didn't wake.

"He's doing well," Rebecca said, shutting the door behind her.

"Yeah, he is," Jordan agreed. He slipped his phone into his pocket, but the device might as well have been burning a hole in the fabric after what he'd read on it.

"Your girlfriend is in the waiting room," Rebecca said with a smile. "Sally tucked a blanket around her because she'd fallen asleep. She's tuckered out."

His heart pulsed as he thanked the nurse and asked him to pass on the gesture to the charge nurse, Sally. He'd seen the hours Abby had been pulling, knew that she was working hard for Hunter and wanting to be there for him. He also knew that she was the most golden-hearted person he'd ever met.

It didn't make sense.

Why would she sell out RoboTech?

Why, after all of the hours she'd spent on design, would she give the information to RoboTech's number one enemy?

To Roberts Enterprises.

She wouldn't.

Abby didn't have any love lost for her father, and she'd been damn loyal to Jordan, to Heather, to Rich.

She wouldn't betray him.

He pushed through the double doors that led out into in the waiting room, holding on to the notion.

Please let that thought be the correct one.

Abby was curled up in a chair, laptop perched on her knees. The screen was black, but she shifted, her fingers brushing the mouse pad. A document came to life, a spreadsheet with rows and rows of information.

Jordan frowned, snagging the laptop before it hit the floor when she moved again, unconsciously seeking a more comfortable position in the rigid wooden chair.

Several lines were highlighted in yellow, and a column on the far right was titled "Me" and filled with periodic "Xs."

Other lines were highlighted in red. And still more in blue, with question marks corresponding in the "Me" column.

He studied the rest of the sheet, trying to make sense of the information. It was mostly numbers: time stamps, length of time, IP addresses.

"Jordan?" Abby asked, her voice hesitant.

He lowered the laptop and stared at her. "What's this?"

Her face went pale and his gut clenched. Dammit, had he been wrong?

"Jordan—" she began. "It's not like you're thinking. I—uh—well. It's complicated . . ."

His stomach sank further and further with each stumbling word.

"—my father, he said—"

Jordan shut his eyes. Breathed. Then opened them.

Of course.

"I need to go." He dropped the laptop onto the chair next to her and walked away.

"Jordan!"

Footsteps echoed down the tile floor.

"Wait."

He yanked open the door to the stairs and rushed down. His feelings were a tangled knot. He didn't know how to coax them free. Abby couldn't have—

His feet stopped at the bottom of the first flight.

But she hadn't denied anything. She hadn't—

No. He shook his head. This wasn't the time to draw out motivations. He needed to sleep. He needed to think.

But he couldn't walk away. *Dammit.* It wasn't that easy.

Jordan couldn't walk away from Abby.

The door at the top of the stairs flew open, and Abby ran through. Her eyes were wild and there were tears on her cheeks. She'd left the computer, her purse, *everything* behind.

And that was the moment he knew for sure.

She'd left it all behind.

For him.

"I didn't!" She gasped out, sliding to a stop at the top of the stairs. "That was what I was trying to say. Someone was logging in under my name, accessing Hunter's project. Heather and I have been tracking it since last week." Abby sank to the top step, sighing as she put her head in her hands. "But I didn't expect that my own father would try to betray me."

Jordan walked up the steps and sat next to her. "Your father hates my family."

"Why?" Abby asked, glancing up at him. "I don't understand how hate could turn him against his own daughter. I didn't want to believe it. Then I saw the press release and knew . . ." One tear slid down her cheek. "What could make him do that to me?"

Jordan brushed a hair back from her face and told her, "My father seduced your mother."

She rolled her eyes and he blinked, surprised.

"It's true."

"I don't doubt it. Just know that my mother had more affairs than a tabloid queen. If my father tried to ruin all the other men in her life, he wouldn't have time to actually run a business."

Jordan put his hands up. "I don't pretend to understand it, all I know is that after my mom died, they were . . . close."

"Ick."

He winced. "Yeah."

Abby sucked in a breath then released it. "I didn't betray you," she whispered.

"I know."

Her eyes went to his. "You do?"

He nodded. "I admit, I freaked for a second, but"—he reached for her hand—"I know you, sweetheart. I was coming back when you barreled through that door like a charging bull."

She glared, but her lips were twitching. "I'm going to let the bovine joke slip for now, but know that in a few more months that'll get you throat punched."

He laughed, wrapped his arms around her. "I love you, Abigail Roberts."

She dropped her forehead to his shoulder and hugged him back. "I love you too, Thor, God of Thunder." A pause. "And your hammer."

Right there in the hospital stairwell, four days before Christmas, he tugged Abby into his lap and kissed her.

And when she told him about the trap she and Heather had laid to trip up the corporate spies, he kissed her again.

Then once more, just for good measure.

THIRTY-ONE

Abby

JORDAN WAS ASLEEP BESIDE ME, sprawled amongst the pillows and comforter, but I was wide awake, my laptop open and at the ready. I just needed to click the button that would upload the final layer to the trap.

I could only hope they would take the bait.

That *my father* would take the bait.

Christmas Eve and I was trying to screw over dear old Dad. Now *that* was the spirit of the season.

Not that he hadn't tried to screw me over first.

Which was the part I didn't understand. Why bother with such a small project when Roberts Enterprises had so much already? It was a nothing product for RoboTech as it was, quite literally Jordan's pet project for Hunter.

So why would my father bother taking it on?

The only reason I could comprehend was revenge.

Ruining a company's reputation for little more than vengeance. It wasn't like I could say it was the first time I'd heard that particular notion.

It's just that . . . I'd thought my father was better than that.

Sighing, I closed the laptop and picked up my phone, texting Heather to let her know the final trap was planted.

I was giving the family of my father's greatest enemy enough material to blackmail him for years. And I was doing it without a second thought.

Because I trusted Heather and Jordan.

Because this all needed to stop.

Because, dammit, I had to believe my father might have a slice of good in him. Despite my childhood, despite the bullying attitude, despite the neglect and distance and disapproval.

My dad had to love me.

Right?

I went into the bathroom and closed the door, leaning back against it for a moment before I turned on the taps to fill the big tub. We were staying at the nicest hotel in town, which happened to be located just a few blocks from the hospital. It was a convenient location and though I'd argued with Jordan about the unnecessary expense of reserving the Presidential Suite, considering we were hardly in it, I was definitely feeling the tub right in that moment.

There were perks to dating a billionaire.

I filled the bath with warm—*not hot*—water and stripped down. I was just about to step in when my phone rang.

Thinking it was Heather, I answered without looking at the caller ID.

Big mistake.

"Abigail."

My father.

"Hi, Dad." I was proud of myself. My voice was steady.

"What have you done?" he hissed.

"I don't know what you're talking about," I said, wondering if he'd come clean and admit to screwing with his daughter's career for ego or revenge or whatever. I wondered if he'd finally tell me why I meant less to him than my brother.

"I should have known," he said, completely obliterating the last bit of hope I'd held for him, "that *you* would do something like this."

I grabbed a towel, wrapped it around myself. "Something like what, Dad?"

"Don't call me that," he spat. "As if I'd want someone like you to—"

My fingers clenched on the towel. "Call you what?" I whispered, but it was apparently enough to cut through his tirade.

"I'm not your father, Abigail," he said, voice icy cold. "I may have given you my name, but I've never acted like a father to you. God knows you should have gotten a fucking clue."

I swallowed. "What are you saying?"

"Little idiot," he snapped. "I'm telling you that I am *not* your father."

A frigid calm swept down my spine. "Who is?"

"A fucking yoga instructor your whore of a mother slept with in Maui. Can you believe it? She tried to come to me, to get me to fuck her. Probably thought she could hide the truth, but I knew. I knew! She—"

I breathed out slowly, trying, one, to come to terms with my Star-Wars-Luke-I-am-your-father-moment and, two, to thank my lucky stars that Jordan wasn't my brother.

That would have been the flipping twist to end all twists in the sordid tale that was my childhood.

"So why didn't you divorce her?"

He scoffed. "Robertses do not divorce. I wasn't about to pay her half of everything just because she couldn't keep her legs closed."

"Wow," I said. "I would have thought that a Roberts wouldn't get married without a prenup."

"Prenups are a requirement *now*. Believe me."

I sat down, leaned back against the tub. "I don't know if I can believe anything you say," I said.

"I think that's my line."

I ignored the quip and instead asked, "Why didn't you send me away? If you hate me so much, why keep me in your life?"

"I don't hate you," he said, then his voice went hard. "Or I didn't until you pulled your little stunt today."

I shrugged even though he couldn't see it. "Hopefully that will teach you not to take things that aren't yours."

"I've got some of the best coders in the industry."

"*Some*, I think, is the key word," I shot back. "RoboTech has the absolute best working on this and"—I pulled my phone from my ear to check the time—"I'd open my email in about five minutes. I think you'll be canceling that release."

"What did you do?"

"Let's just say, if you're pissed now, I expect a monumental explosion when you open that email." I pressed on when he tried to interrupt, saying, "I don't understand anything about what happened between my mother and you. Why the elaborate gifts and birthday parties?" I laughed though it wasn't humor-filled. "I guess I understand why you were so forceful when it came to sending me away to boarding school after she left. But everything beyond that, I don't get. Why the job offer? Why the trust fund? Why pay for college?"

He was quiet for so long that I thought he'd hung up.

"Money is the easy part," he said. "Emotions are too complicated."

"That's it?" I asked when he didn't say anything else.

"That's it."

Wow. Somehow, that didn't make me feel any better. No wonder my mother . . . *no*. That wasn't an excuse, no matter how cold and difficult my father—*Bernie*—was. There wasn't a justifiable reason for parading through lives and men and marriages, wreaking havoc as she pranced.

There was no reason to leave me behind.

"I guess I won't be over for Christmas tomorrow," I said.

"No. I don't think you should come."

A slice of pain pulsed through my heart.

"For the record," he said. "That trap you and Heather pulled off today was pretty good."

"I almost think that was a compliment," I said, forcing my feelings down and trying to keep my tone light. I could cry later, after I'd digested everything he said. Now, I wouldn't let him hear me crumble. "From the discerning Bernie Roberts. Someone knock me over with a feather." A fake laugh. "Good chat. Can't wait for the next one."

Just before I hung up, he spoke. "You were a beautiful baby, Abs."

Then he was gone.

God, my family was seriously fucked up.

SPENDING CHRISTMAS DAY at the hospital just a little more than a week after spending a birthday unconscious in the *same* hospital wasn't on any kid's wish list, but Hunter was a trooper nonetheless.

He was more alert than the days previous and super excited about the package Jordan brought in.

Which contained a prototype of RoboTech's robot. Complete in shiny, brightly colored packaging that I had designed.

Which looked amazing—but that was just my opinion—so I was extra nervous as he tore open off the Santa print wrapping paper and studied the box.

"A robot!" he said, immediately ignoring all of the painstak- ingly designed details and tearing straight into the cardboard. "Can I make it move?"

Jordan nodded and helped him retrieve the little robot. "You sure can."

"And jump?"

Another nod.

"And talk?"

"Yes," Jordan said. "At least a few words."

I could have waxed poetic to him about the balance and composition, how I'd spent hours looking for the perfect shadow-free image that didn't have the models—a pair of six- year-old twins, one boy and one girl—looking like they were insane, crazed, or trying to murder each other.

But I didn't.

Because his enthusiasm to get inside the packaging was exactly why I'd spent so long creating it.

I didn't want kids to study the box in confusion—to try to figure out what was inside.

I wanted them to know the contents immediately . . . and then be unable to wait another second before tearing it open and playing with that toy.

Hunter doing just that pleased me beyond belief.

However, there was one detail he'd missed in his enthusiasm that I wanted to make sure he noticed.

That the little girl inside me, who'd felt so lonely and discarded, *needed* to make sure he understood. Because he was special and good and sweet and even though his father was gone and his mother had left, he still deserved to know that he was loved.

That Jordan loved him.

And that I loved him too, but that portion of the story could wait until another day.

Jordan was installing the batteries as I rounded the bed and started scooping up the paper and cardboard.

"Hey," I said, holding a piece up to Hunter. "Whose name is that?"

He frowned, little blond brows coming together for a half second before his eyes went wide. "That's *my* name!"

Jordan nodded. "Yeah, bud, it is."

"Cool!"

And then Hunter's attention went right back to the robot.

Which was exactly how it should have been.

I tossed the trash into the bin and then went to sit by Cecilia.

"This," I said, reaching into my purse and pulling out a card, "is for you."

"What?" Her eyes widened. "I-I didn't get you anything."

"You didn't have to," I said, closing her fingers around the envelope. "But a little birdie gave me hints about something you might like. And this is open-ended so you can use it when you're ready."

Cecilia's expression was careful. "Uh, okay?"

I smiled. "Okay is good. Just open it. I promise it will make more sense if you do."

She carefully tore open the envelope and pulled out what was inside. It was a round-trip plane ticket to Finland and behind that a voucher for a very special hotel.

Cecilia gasped. "For—"

I nodded. "For the Northern Lights. I heard that you really want to see them."

Her eyes filled with tears, her chin bobbed jerkily. "I-I do. I've always wanted to go, but I can't accept . . ."

Carefully, I closed her fingers around the papers. "You can." I narrowed my eyes at her. "Or rather, you *will*."

"Abby—"

"Shh," I said. "Just hug me and accept. And"—I touched her arm—"promise me that when we're out of the woods here, you'll go."

"I—" She sighed. "I don't know what to say."

"Don't say anything," I told her. "Hugs." I extended my arms, gesturing with my fingers at her to come on and do it already. "Then tuck that envelope into your purse and plan a trip."

"You're stubborn," she said, but hugged me all the same.

"Thank you for being there for Hunter," I whispered. "I don't know what he would have done without you."

"I love him," she said simply.

"And he loves you."

We both sniffed, holding tight until the sound of Hunter's unmistakable giggles reached us. Then we pulled back and gazed over at the boys. They were huddled on the bed, Jordan's arm around Hunter as he showed him how to program the robot.

"He loves him too," Cecilia said. "And you."

"I know." I smiled. "And the feeling is completely mutual."

THIRTY-TWO

Abby

"YOU!" Bec pointed a finger at Jordan, who'd answered the door. It was just after the New Year and we'd been planning a take out and movie night. "You need to shoo. And you"—she turned that finger to me—"need to be sitting on the couch, getting ready to be pampered."

Seraphina stood behind her, arms laden with bags. "Move it, princess," she said, nudging Bec to the side. "You were so worried about your manicure that you couldn't carry the bags, the least you could do is move that big ole butt of yours out of the way."

Bec made to smack her then stopped, flashing me her freshly painted nails. "Gel manicure," she stage-whispered. "I just didn't want to carry the bags."

Seraphina gasped in outrage. "You—"

"Ladies," Jordan interrupted firmly. "What's going on?" His gaze flicked to the doorway again. "Cecilia? Is everything okay?"

She nodded, glancing around uncomfortably. "Hunter's fine. Umm. Bec wouldn't take no for an answer."

"Heather's with Hunter for a few hours," Seraphina said. "Auntie time." She shooed him toward the hall. "Which means that you are going to go see a movie or go to the mall or something."

"What am I going to do at the mall?"

Seraphina rolled her eyes. "I don't know. I don't care. What I *do* care about is sneaking in a few hours of Abby time without you tagging along."

"Hey, that's—"

"We like you, God of Thunder," Bec said, "but you're cramping our style."

"I-uh—" Jordan turned to me and I tried not to smile. I knew my friends, knew they could railroad just about anyone, let alone someone with a soft heart like Jordan. All things considered, I was rather enjoying the show.

"Don't look at me," I said. "I love spending time with you."

Bec made a barfing sound. "Gross."

Jordan shook his head, crossed to the couch—Bec had pushed me down onto the cushions and covered my lap with a blanket. He kissed me, long and slow and deep, leaving me a breathless lump before he pulled away. "I'm coming back in two hours."

I nodded, maybe dumbly, definitely dazed as he climbed the stairs to our bedroom.

"Damn," Seraphina said, setting the stacks of bags on the coffee table. "I think I came just watching that. What happened to Hair-Trigger Hammer?"

I snorted. "Apparently he was just out of practice."

"I'd take some of that *out of practice.*"

We all froze and stared at Cecilia, whose cheeks were bright pink.

"I—uh—" she stammered.

"Told you you'd love her," Bec said to Seraphina, nudging her with her elbow.

"Shh," Seraphina said. "You're being rude."

"*Both* of you are being ridiculous," I said and patted the couch. "Sit over here, Cecilia. I think I smell chocolate."

"We have dark chocolate," Bec said, dropping to her knees to begin unpacking bags. "It's good for the baby."

"And for us," Seraphina said, pulling out a pair of pajamas from a bag and tossing them at Cecilia. "These are for you."

Cecilia's eyes bugged out when she saw the tag. "These—I can't! They're too expensive."

"Girl," Bec said. "Your innuendo now means that we're forever friends and as such, you will accept all gifts of chocolate and ridiculously expensive pajamas forevermore."

I snorted.

"You must have really low standards for friendship," Cecilia muttered.

Then promptly clamped a hand over her mouth.

Seraphina and Bec glanced at each other then at me, bursting into laughter. "Well, that much is obvious," Bec said.

"Hey!" I laughed.

"Oh, my God." Cecilia closed her eyes. "I did not just say that."

"You did." Bec grinned. "Which just proves our friendship standards. We live by three rules: be snarky, make every conversation dirty, and wear extremely pricey but excessively cozy pajamas."

"Now go," Seraphina said. "Bathroom is the third door on the left."

I rolled my eyes at the idea of my best friend giving directions in my house—Cecilia had been over enough times by now to know every nook and cranny—and caught the pair that Seraphina tossed me.

"Maternity edition," she said, brushing her hand over the little bump that was my baby. "Go change."

"I'll help," Jordan quipped, waggling his eyebrows at me as he came back into the room. He'd changed into jeans and put on a jacket.

"I bet you would," Bec cackled. "But we don't have seconds to spare."

Jordan's gaze met mine and he shook his head. Still, his eyes were amused. "Your friends are something else."

I grinned. "I know."

Bec took Jordan's arm and led him to the door to the garage. There she patted his cheeks—the upper then the lower—and shoved him out. "You'll do, Thor. You'll just do," she said as it slammed closed.

Clicking the lock, she turned back toward us. "Okay. I need chocolate and a movie that will make me cry. STAT."

———

Two Weeks Later

"Can we go? Can we go?" Hunter asked, little butt wiggling in his bed. "I'm ready to go home."

Hunter was being discharged today. Finally.

Well, the finally was all him. I personally thought that the stay was too short, that he should be monitored and under watch just to make sure everything was going okay. He had a new heart and so many things could go wrong and—

"Abby!"

I blinked. "Sorry, what?"

"Is it time to go?"

"We just need to wait for the doctor to put in the discharge instructions and we're out of here, bud," Jordan said, gathering up the last of Hunter's things and putting them into a clear plastic bag. "I'll run these to the car. You two good?"

Hunter sighed. "I want to go home."

"I know, honey," I said, signaling to Jordan that we were fine. "Unfortunately, these things sometimes just take time."

He scowled. "Where's CeCe?"

"At home, getting everything all ready for you."

Another sigh, but he turned back to the robot, tinkering again, adding more details, tweaking the programing—not that he would call it that. The Hunter robot was just learning a new trick. But I could see why it was the perfect toy for real life Hunter.

Something that would keep him semi-stationary.

It was hard to tell he'd even had a transplant just not even two months before. I'd never really realized how sick he was, how pale-gray and weak, until compared to this version of Hunter.

Healthy and pink-skinned.

"I want to come with you and Jordan," he said.

"Soon," I told him.

We needed to be within a half hour of the hospital and its transplant center for a few more months. Then Hunter would move into my—to *our*—house.

"But we'll visit every day," I said. "And Jordan will be there and—"

"Yeah."

I frowned. "What's going on, honey?"

"I—" Pale blue eyes filled with tears. "Are you going to leave, too?"

My heart clenched, but I forced my voice to stay calm. "No, honey. I'm afraid you're stuck with me."

"Okay," he said, but the word wasn't confident.

I wished there was something I could say that would make him believe that I was going to be around for the long haul, that I loved him too much already to possibly think about leaving and never coming back.

But I knew from personal experience it wasn't that easy.

Once a child's trust was truly broken . . . well, some things couldn't be repaired.

There were always cracks, valleys that never quite healed.

"Did you know my mom left too?" I asked, brushing back his hair.

His eyes flew up to mine, surprised.

"I was sad for a long time," I said. "But eventually I realized she hadn't left because of me."

Hunter's gaze fell to the bed. "If I hadn't gotten sick . . ."

I wrapped my arms tightly around him and said the only thing I could. "It's not your fault."

He shuddered, sniffed, and I held on.

"Sometimes things in life really suck. Sometimes things aren't fair. Sometimes people are mean." I pressed a kiss to his head. "But that's the time to hold on to people who are nice, who love you, and who see you for the awesome, wonderful eight-year-old you are."

Hunter's little arms wrapped around my waist. "I do have a robot named after me."

I smiled, feeling tears well in my eyes. "That you do."

My stomach fluttered and I gasped, pressing my hand to it.

"What?" Hunter asked, pulling back.

"It's nothing," I said, trying to memorize the feeling. It was the baby moving. I knew it. I felt that in the depths of my soul. And the tears that had been welling escaped from the corners of my eyes.

"Abby?"

"I'm fine," I said, dashing them away. I cried at cleaning

commercials lately, so it wasn't a surprise that feeling my baby for the first time made me teary. But I didn't want to make Hunter worry.

"Is it the baby?"

My jaw dropped open. We hadn't mentioned one word about the pregnancy, not wanting to add another layer of stress to the already stressful situation for Hunter. He'd been through so much that I didn't want him to think Jordan would drop him for a new baby.

But apparently, we hadn't been so good at hiding the fact that I was pregnant.

"The baby is fine," I quickly assured him when I saw the worried look on his face. "I just felt him or her move for the first time."

"Maybe it was my voice," Hunter said with a grin. "I bet he likes me already."

"That's a guarantee," I said, head spinning a bit with the speed of Hunter's conversational U-turns. "What makes you think the baby will be a boy?"

He lifted his chin. "I know."

"Okay," I said and stood. "Should I go see if we can hurry this process up a bit?"

"Yes!"

"Oh. Hunter?" I paused in the doorway. "How did you know about the baby?"

He gave me a look that was way too mature for someone his age. "I'm eight, Abby. I know things." A pause. "I hope Uncle Jordan marries you."

My breath caught as Hunter began tinkering with the robot again and I left the room thinking the child was right.

He knew things . . . *way* too many things.

I made a vow right then and there that he would know less of the adult—less hospitals, less family drama, less pain, and fear. I made a vow to let him get dirty, to help him make friends his age, to play football with him in the backyard, to break windows with foul balls, and stink up the laundry room with his shoes.

I made a vow to love that little boy like my own.

EPILOGUE

Jordan, Four Months Later

JORDAN SLID CAREFULLY from the bed and tucked the covers up under Abby's chin. Her brow puckered and he pressed a kiss there, loving the way the lines relaxed at his touch.

He loved everything about her, in fact.

Which was what today was about.

It was Abby's first Mother's Day, and he and Hunter had a hell of a day planned.

Well, it technically revolved around pajamas, cuddling on the couch, and watching cheesy movies.

Carter whimpered again, and Jordan turned to their week-old son, feeling his heart expand to the size of a watermelon. It was amazing how so much love could grow in a second, with a single glance, with only one touch.

People who didn't believe in love at first sight must not have had kids.

"Shh," he said softly, scooping him up and slipping from the room before the noise could wake Abby. She'd been up feeding him every two hours the night before and deserved a break.

As much as he wanted to help her, he didn't have the right parts. So aside from changing diapers and walking the halls with Carter to get him to settle, he couldn't do much to relieve the exhaustion that Abby must be feeling.

Hell, he felt half dead and he had hardly done anything.

Jordan walked down the hall and into the kitchen, putting a pot of coffee on to brew as he smiled down at his son.

Rosy cheeks, blue eyes that matched his own—he thought they would stay blue, though Abby thought they'd turn hazel—and wispy brown hair.

He was a squishy faced, chunky, little lump.

And Jordan loved him more than life itself.

"You're pretty special," he said. "Did you know that?" Wide eyes stared up at him, and he kept talking. Carter was probably hungry, but he wanted to give Abby as much sleep as possible.

He'd avoid waking her until he had to.

"You're so lucky. Your Mommy and I both love you very much, and you have a brother who's crazy about you." Jordan touched Carter's nose, smiling when his son rooted around. His delay tactics may not last long. "Because that's what Hunter is to you," he said, blabbering on against the losing battle anyway. "You're more than just cousins. You're brothers."

"Uncle Jordan?"

He looked up at the sound of Hunter's voice. It was as sleepy as his rumpled appearance—jammies wrinkled, hair askew.

"Yeah, bud?"

"Is that true?"

Jordan bounced Carter. "Is what true?"

"Is he really my brother?"

"Come here," he said, patting the barstool. "Family is a

tricky thing. People get hung up on moms and dads and who is technically related to whom. But I don't think any of that matters." He held up Carter, who locked eyes on Hunter, the same way he did every time Hunter was in the room. "All I know is that Carter is going to need a big brother. That he's going to need lots of people in his life to love him." He wrapped one arm around Hunter's shoulders. "Just the same as you."

"I think I'd make a good big brother," Hunter said.

Jordan grinned. "I know you will. Window-breaker."

"It was an accident!" Hunter hung his head. "I didn't realize that it would . . ."

Jordan raised a brow. "Break? If you hit a ball really hard?" He nudged him. "I thought Abby would lose a gasket."

Hunter nodded emphatically. "Me too."

Instead, all she'd done was smile, shake her head, and tell Jordan to call someone to fix it.

Carter let out another squawk, this one more determined and louder.

"I think Mommy's time is up," Jordan said. "While Abby is feeding Carter, let's get everything ready, okay?"

"Okay!" Hunter nodded and ran off in the direction of the living room. "I'll get the pajamas!"

He stared down at Carter, his first biological son but the second son of his heart. "I love that kid."

Carter cooed.

Jordan crossed the kitchen, opened the cabinet above the fridge—the one Abby deemed as unusable because she was so short—and pulled out the little box he'd stashed within.

Pajamas. Chocolate. Bad movies. Check. Check. Check.

He stashed the ring in her basket of yarn and set it on the coffee table as Hunter ran like a tornado gathering the pajamas and a cozy blanket and turning on the T.V.

"Good?" he asked.

Hunter gave him a thumbs-up and Jordan turned down the hall, cuddling Carter close as he walked. Carefully, he turned the knob and crept into the bedroom, wanting to wake Abby gently.

But she was already up, eyes heavy, hair crazy, and more beautiful than anyone else on the planet.

"Hey," he said.

She smiled. "Hey, honey."

"Someone is hungry," he said. "I tried to delay him, but I wasn't successful."

"Tell that to my boobs." She pointed to the part of her body that had grown to rival Seraphina's set and grimaced. "They apparently know that Carter is hungry."

He set Carter in her arms. "I'm going to take a quick shower while you feed him."

In reality, he was taking a quick shower for two reasons: one, boobs—as in, hers were on display and giant and he wanted to touch them, but he couldn't—and two, he was nervous about proposing.

Which was ridiculous. They'd discussed marriage. They were planning on adopting Hunter, had just had a kid together.

It was a sure thing.

And he didn't want to screw it up.

"Okay," she said, her focus on Carter.

Probably a good thing, otherwise she would have seen that he was a mess.

Ten minutes later, he was clean and ready. Hunter knocked on the bedroom door as Jordan emerged from the bathroom in fresh clothes . . . or fresh pajamas. He glanced at Abby, who nodded. Carter had finished eating. He reached for the knob—

"Happy Mother's Day!" Hunter announced, launching himself on the bed.

Jordan shook his head. The boy never walked when sprinting would do.

"Thanks, sweetie," Abby said, hugging him with her free arm. "Did you sleep okay?"

"Yup. Here." He dropped the package on the bed. "These are for you. Jordan and I planned a day with your favorite things."

Her eyes rose to meet Jordan's. He nodded. "Chocolate. Hallmark movies. The works." One side of his mouth quirked. "We'll even let you have a shower first."

"My heroes," she quipped and slid from the bed. "Or maybe you're saying that I *need* a shower?"

"Definitely."

She snorted, rose on tiptoe to press a kiss to his lips. "Thanks for that." A glint in mischievous hazel eyes. "Do I need to bust out the hammer jokes?"

"God, no." He took Carter from her. "Enjoy your uninterrupted shower," he told her. "I've got the boys."

"I love you," she whispered.

"Right back at you."

Shaking her head, she went into the bathroom. Hunter helped him change Carter—or rather picked out fresh clothes while Jordan dealt with the *nasty* diaper business, as Hunter liked to call it.

By the time they'd gotten Carter settled and Hunter a bowl of cereal for breakfast, Abby was done with her shower.

Hunter dropped his bowl in the sink when she came into the kitchen. "Come this way!" He took her hand, dragging her into the family room.

Jordan's heart skipped a beat and he wiped sweaty palms on his shirt. "This is it, bud," he whispered to Carter. "I hope she says yes."

Carter blinked up at him.

"I know." Jordan laughed. "I'll be lucky if she does."

He walked into the next room, smiling when he saw Hunter fussing over Abby—arranging the pillows behind her back, positioning the remote at just the right distance. He met Jordan's eyes and nodded at the basket, a nonverbal cue to get moving.

"Can I hold Carter?" he asked, moving to the armchair and sitting down, arms extended.

"Sure, bud," Jordan said, helping him to settle back and support Carter's head.

Abby's eyes were soft. "They're so sweet together," she said, watching Hunter hold Carter.

"Yes, they are." He reached for the basket, opened his mouth—

"And *this* is sweet," she said. "You guys are going to spoil me. How did you get these chocolates? I've never seen them anywhere except in Switzerland."

He shrugged. "I flew them in. Abby—"

"You *flew* them in?" She gasped. "That must have been ridiculously expensive."

"I wanted to make today special."

"It would have been special without chocolate." Jordan lifted a brow and she grinned. "Okay maybe not."

"Abby"—he went down on one knee next to the coffee table—"I wanted to ask if you would—"

"Oh, my God. Is that new yarn?" She clapped her hands together before reaching for the basket. "It's gorgeous."

"*Abby.*" He caught her hands before she could grab it. "Shush for a second, okay?"

She blinked.

"I'm trying to ask you something."

Her eyes drifted from the basket in his hands to his position on one knee.

"A-are you—?"

"Yup." He held up the basket. "I wanted to ask if you would crochet with me."

There was one beat of silence before she smacked him in the chest. "Jordan O'Keith, so help me . . ."

He pulled out the box and set the basket down. "Abigail Roberts. We've done this all sorts of backward, but I can't imagine spending my life without you. Will you marry me?"

The box made a little creak as he opened it, showing off what was an obscenely-sized princess cut diamond ring inside. But he'd never had any restraint when it came to Abby, and he'd definitely not had any when it came to the ring she was going to wear for the rest of her life.

"No."

Or maybe not.

"What?" He set the box down, took her hand. "It's okay if it's too soon. I just—"

She laughed, yanking him close. "I'm sorry, I couldn't resist." She kissed him. "I would be honored to be your wife."

He kissed her long enough to warrant a "gross" from Hunter and pulled back to slip the ring on her finger. "I'm going to pay you back for that one," he said.

Her hand came up to cup his cheek. "I hope so," she murmured. "For the rest of our lives."

And he kissed her again, ignoring the retching sound Hunter made.

He had his happily ever after, dammit, and he was going to enjoy it.

Thank you for reading! I hope you loved meeting Abby and Jordan! The next book in the Billionaire's Club series is BAD

BREAKUP. Find out what happens when the man sitting next to her on a plane turns out to be CeCe's ex...

CLICK HERE TO READ BAD BREAKUP NOW >

And if you enjoyed BAD NIGHT STAND, you'll love the sexy, sweet, and close-knit Breakers Hockey crew. The first book in the series, BROKEN, is now live!

The more she falls for Stefan, the more she risks her career... Don't miss the Gold Hockey series. It begins with the over 400 five-star-reviewed BLOCKED!

"Off-the-charts hot, smexy scenes with one of the best book boyfriends I have come across!" —Amazon reviewer

DOWNLOAD BLOCKED FOR FREE >

I so appreciate your help in spreading the word about my books, including sharing with friends! Please leave a review on your favorite book site!
You can also join my Facebook group, the Fabinators, for exclusive giveaways and sneak peeks of future books.

SIGN UP FOR ELISE FABER'S NEWSLETTER HERE:
https://www.elisefaber.com/newsletter

Excerpt from BAD BREAKUP

Cecilia sat on the plane, her first class seat luxurious and insanely comfortable. It might have been the first time in her limited travel experience that she didn't feel like cattle shoved into the back of a truck, and instead like an actual person with wants and needs.

"Your champagne, Ms. Thiele."

"Thank you," she said and took a sip, leaning back into the butter-soft leather with a sigh.

She'd just closed her eyes when someone sat down in the empty seat next to her.

Rustling accompanied the movement as the person got settled.

"Can I get you anything?" the flight attendant asked.

"A whiskey."

The hairs stood up on Cecilia's neck. Oh, God no. It couldn't possibly be—

She clenched her lids tightly, refusing, absolutely refusing to open them. No. She was hearing things. It had been years since she'd heard that voice.

Too many years.

"Here you go, Mr. McGregor."

Oh fuck.

Her eyes flew open, she peeked out, and dread twisted her stomach into knots.

No. It couldn't be.

She'd booked this flight last minute, deciding to use the voucher from Abby after she and Jordan had returned from their honeymoon. Cecilia's life had felt stagnant. She'd needed to get away, and she'd had the free flight and hotel.

It made sense to use it, however last minute.

Plus, everything had worked out. There had been one first class seat open. Only one cabin at her dream resort.

And now she was sitting next to Colin McGregor.

"Flight attendants, arm the doors," the pilot's voice chimed through the plane's speakers.

A thud signaled her last avenue of retreat disappearing.

She was trapped on a nonstop flight for twelve hours. With the man who'd left her at the altar.

How was this possibly her life?

"Cecilia?" that masculine voice asked. "Is that really you?"

And just like all the times before, her eyes were drawn to him. She'd never been able to ignore him. Not Colin. Not even when he'd—

But this time was different.

She wasn't weak. She wasn't a vulnerable girl in a rough place.

She'd been through hell and back.

Colin had no power over her.

Not anymore.

Cecilia put in her earbuds and turned her back on the man who'd devastated her world five years before.

Want a free bonus story? Hate missing Elise's new releases?
Love contests, exclusive excerpts and giveaways?
Then signup for Elise's newsletter here!
https://www.elisefaber.com/newsletter

And join Elise's fan group, the Fabinators https://www.facebook.com/groups/fabinators for insider information, sneak peaks at new releases, and fun freebies! Hope to see you there!

BILLIONAIRE'S CLUB

Bad Night Stand
Bad Breakup
Bad Husband
Bad Hookup
Bad Divorce
Bad Fiancé
Bad Boyfriend
Bad Blind Date
Bad Wedding
Bad Engagement
Bad Bridesmaid
Bad Swipe
Bad Girlfriend
Bad Best Friend
Bad Billionaire's Quickies

ALSO BY ELISE FABER

Billionaire's Club (all stand alone)

Bad Night Stand

Bad Breakup

Bad Husband

Bad Hookup

Bad Divorce

Bad Fiancé

Bad Boyfriend

Bad Blind Date

Bad Wedding

Bad Engagement

Bad Bridesmaid

Bad Swipe

Bad Girlfriend

Bad Best Friend

Bad Billionaire's Quickies

Gold Hockey (all stand alone)

Blocked

Backhand

Boarding

Benched

Breakaway

Breakout

Checked

Coasting

Centered

Charging

Caged

Crashed

A Gold Christmas

Cycled

Caught (February 1,2022)

Breakers Hockey (all stand alone)

Broken

Boldly

Breathless

Ballsy (April 26,2022)

Love, Action, Camera (all stand alone)

Dotted Line

Action Shot

Close-Up

End Scene

Meet Cute

Love After Midnight (all stand alone)

Rum And Notes

Virgin Daiquiri

On The Rocks

Sex On The Seats

Life Sucks Series (all stand alone)

Train Wreck

Hot Mess

Dumpster Fire

Clusterf*@k

FUBAR (March 29,2022)

Roosevelt Ranch Series (all stand alone, series complete)

Disaster at Roosevelt Ranch

Heartbreak at Roosevelt Ranch

Collision at Roosevelt Ranch

Regret at Roosevelt Ranch

Desire at Roosevelt Ranch

Phoenix Series (read in order)

Phoenix Rising

Dark Phoenix

Phoenix Freed

Phoenix: LexTal Chronicles (rereleasing soon, stand alone, Phoenix world)

From Ashes

In Flames

To Smoke

KTS Series

Riding The Edge

Crossing The Line

Leveling The Field

Scorching The Earth (January 25,2022)

Cocky Heroes World

Tattooed Troublemaker

ACKNOWLEDGMENTS

ACKNOWLEDGEMENTS

Thank you for reading Bad Night Stand! I hope you enjoyed Jordan and Abby's story, as it's one I seriously loved writing! If you'd like to catch up on all my other releases, please check out my website: www.elisefaber.com. There you can sign up for my newsletter (with monthly bookish giveaways, woohoo!), check out my other books (everything from paranormal romance to hockey romance to contemporary stand alones), and get to know more about my dorky self (hockey, chocolate, Star Wars . . . okay, I'm pretty boring).

You can also find me on Facebook (@elisefaberauthor), via my FB fan group (facebook.com/group/fabinators), or Instagram (@elisefaber). I look forward to talking with you soon!

-XOXO,

Elise

ABOUT THE AUTHOR

USA Today bestselling author, Elise Faber, loves chocolate, Star Wars, Harry Potter, and hockey (the order depending on the day and how well her team -- the Sharks! -- are playing). She and her husband also play as much hockey as they can squeeze into their schedules, so much so that their typical date night is spent on the ice. Elise is the mom to two exuberant boys and lives in Northern California. Connect with her in her Facebook group, the Fabinators or find more information about her books at www.elisefaber.com.

[f] facebook.com/elisefaberauthor

[a] amazon.com/author/elisefaber

[BB] bookbub.com/profile/elise-faber

[O] instagram.com/elisefaber

[g] goodreads.com/elisefaber

[P] pinterest.com/elisefaberwrite

Made in the USA
Columbia, SC
10 July 2024

38462327R00157